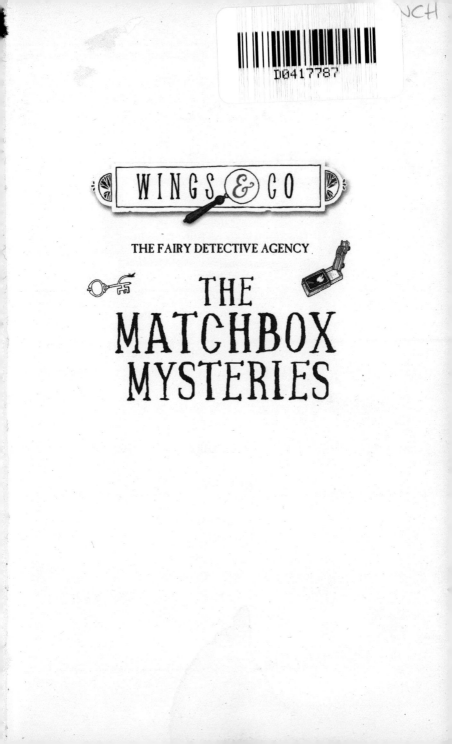

WINGS & CO

THE FAIRY DETECTIVE AGENCY

THE MATCHBOX MYSTERIES

SALLY GARDNER

Illustrated by

David Roberts

WINGS & CO

THE FAIRY DETECTIVE AGENCY

THE MATCHBOX MYSTERIES

Orion
Children's Books

First published in Great Britain in 2014
by Orion Children's Books
a division of the Orion Publishing Group Ltd
Orion House
5 Upper St Martin's Lane
London WC2H 9EA
A Hachette UK Company

1 3 5 7 9 10 8 6 4 2

A catalogue record for this book is available from the British Library.

ISBN 978 1 4440 1014 5

Printed and bound in Great Britain
by Clays Ltd, St Ives plc

The Orion Publishing Group's policy is to use papers that are natural,
renewable and recyclable products made from wood grown in sustainable
forests. The logging and manufacturing processes are expected to
conform to the environmental regulations of the country of origin.

www.orionbooks.co.uk

To my amazing brother Charlie

With all my love

SG

Chapter One

NO FIBS FROM PHIBBS
The Best Deals On Four Wheels

S o read the sign over Podgy Bottom's car showroom.
The owner, Preston Phibbs, was proudly polishing
a red 1957 Ford Thunderbird convertible when a giant
silhouette of a man with broad shoulders and a hat struck
the showroom floor.

Preston Phibbs felt a strange chill run down his spine.

'Hello,' he called out. 'Hello there, can I help you?'

The silhouette fell across the car's cream soft-top.

From nowhere came a voice with a bad American
accent. 'Gee, getta load of those wheels – black and white
with silver hubcaps.'

'Yes, quite,' replied Preston Phibbs, nervously twiddling
his moustache. He still couldn't make out where the voice
was coming from.

'Those hooded headlights are hot,' it said. 'This baby's got the best chrome smile I've ever seen.'

Preston Phibbs still couldn't see who was talking. He nearly jumped out of his skin when he felt a presence behind him.

He looked round to find a man who was dressed like a gangster from an old black-and-white movie. His fedora hat was pulled over dark glasses to meet a large bow tie, so that apart from a rather red nose, his face was hidden from view. His double-breasted suit was so padded at the shoulders that the man appeared almost square in shape. On his feet he wore very pointed black-and-white two-tone shoes.

'We are about to close,' said Preston Phibbs.

'Then I'm just in time. I'm gonna take that car home with me,' said the man, pointing at the Ford Thunderbird convertible.

Preston Phibbs had worked long enough as a car salesman to know that it was a mistake to judge a man by an ill-fitting gangster suit.

'This car, sir, is one of the finest examples of its kind and costs eighty-five thousand pounds.'

'I don't do zeros,' said the man.

'Oh, very witty, sir,' said Preston Phibbs. He smiled. Of course. Hallowe'en was just over a week away and there was to be a Hallowe'en Ball at the Red Lion Hotel. That's why the chap was dressed as a gangster. He must belong to one of the acts. 'Are you anything to do with the bash at the Red Lion Hotel this Hallowe'en?'

'Bash? Yep, I'm always ready for one of those,' said the man, as he walked round the car, stopping to cup his hands and stare through the window at the red steering wheel. As he bent forward, Preston Phibbs saw, to his alarm, something bulky under his jacket. 'It's swell. I wannit,' said the man.

'I'm afraid I'm about to close,' repeated Preston Phibbs. He fiddled with his mobile phone. This customer was beginning to worry him.

'Let's just settle this right now,' said the man, and took out of his pocket not a cheque book or a credit card, but a matchbox.

'We are closing,' said Preston Phibbs, feeling somewhat

hot under the collar.
'Why don't you come
back tomorrow morning,
sir?'

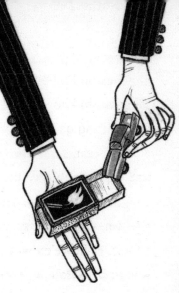

'I don't do tomorrows.
I do the HERE and the NOW,'
said the man. He pulled a huge
plastic water pistol from under
his double-breasted jacket.

Preston Phibbs laughed heartily in
relief.

'That'll go down well at the Hallowe'en Ball. You must
be one of the star acts that I've read about. A magician
maybe?' he said.

'You could say that,' said the man, and fired the water
pistol at the Thunderbird.

'Oh, no. Spare me the waterworks,' said Preston Phibbs.
'I've just polished . . .'

But before he could say another word, the red 1957
Ford Thunderbird convertible began to shrink. Speechless,
Preston Phibbs watched as the solution to his cash-flow
problems became smaller and smaller, until it was so small
that the man picked it up and put it in the matchbox.

By the time Preston Phibbs had recovered from the
shock of what had just happened, all he could see of

the man was his huge shadow disappearing out of the showroom door.

With shaky fingers, he called Podgy Bottom Police Station. Sergeant Litton answered the phone.

'One of my cars has been shrunk – no, I mean one of my cars has been stolen,' cried Preston Phibbs. 'Shrunk. Stolen.'

This wasn't the first odd call that Sergeant Litton had received that day. In the morning, a man had been taken to Podgy Bottom Hospital's A&E swearing that he had seen his Rolls Royce shrunk to matchbox size. That afternoon, a woman had phoned from the local branch of Slugbury's supermarket to say she had witnessed the same thing happen to her four-wheel drive.

Sergeant Litton arrived at Preston Phibbs's showroom at about half past five. The car salesman's face was whiter than an ice rink.

'What do I do now?' he said. 'That car was going to solve my money problems.'

'Tell me in your own words what happened,' said the sergeant.

'My red 1957 Ford Thunderbird convertible shrank before my eyes,' wailed the car salesman.

He was interrupted by the showroom jingle, which was timed to sing out on the hour, every hour.

No fibs
From Phibbs.
The Best Deals
On Four Wheels.

'Eighty-five thousand pounds of prime car gone. Shrunk to the size of a matchbox.'

'Are you sure, sir?' said Sergeant Litton.

'Yes!' shouted Preston Phibbs. 'Yes – and for once I am telling the truth.'

Chapter Two

Wings & Co's shop had been built, as you most probably know, on four long iron legs. At the bottom of the legs were three griffin's talons with steel claws, which meant that the shop, if it felt like it, could dig itself out of its foundations and walk to a different part of the world. And that is exactly how Fidget the cat, Emily Vole, and Buster Ignatius Spicer – plus the magic lamp, the keys and Doughnut the dog, of course – had all found themselves that summer in Puddliepool-on-Sea.

Having solved the mystery of the vanishing of the giant, Billy Buckle, and reunited him with his daughter, the detectives decided they deserved a well-earned rest. Or, as Fidget put it, a holiday.

Emily Vole had never had one of those before.

'What will we do on this holiday?' asked Emily.

Fidget was standing at the shop door wearing a straw hat, a cream linen suit and canvas shoes. In other words, every centimetre of his one hundred and eighty-three was looking very dapper.

'We will,' he said, 'build sandcastles, fly kites, eat fish and chips, go crabbing, paddle in the sea, ride donkeys, eat candy-floss and that's just for starters, my little ducks. Did I mention fish and chips?'

It didn't take long for Emily to find out that this holiday business was really very enjoyable. She had almost forgotten they were supposed to be running a detective agency.

Buster, who since a previous experience in the desert hadn't been that keen on sand, took a shine to it. He discovered he could build almost anything, mixed with the right amount of sea water. He built the Taj Mahal and won the sandcastle competition. A local reporter came to interview him and asked if he had copied it from a picture. Buster loved 'pat on the head' questions.

'Oh, it was nothing really,' he said. 'I suppose it helps if you saw the original being built.'

The reporter smiled. She liked children with imagination.

'And when was that?' she asked.

'1632, when the emperor lost his wife. It was a very sad time all round,' said Buster.

The reporter left that bit out. All that appeared in the paper was a picture of Buster with the Taj Mahal sandcastle.

The magic lamp was the only one who wouldn't go down to the beach. The keys had enjoyed running round and rolling in the sand, but the lamp had decided that sea water and metal didn't mix. The lamp's appearance on the TV show The Me Moment had given it a taste of fame and it felt it had a duty to keep its complexion rust-free. If it was to take its theatrical career further, it needed to be in tip-top condition, so while everyone else was enjoying the seaside the magic lamp set off to the local gym.

As with all holidays, the wind finally changed.

Emily became aware that the weather was a little colder and that the summer was packing up shop. The children had long since gone back to school, the beach was deserted, the donkeys had returned to their winter quarters, and the ice-cream sellers were closing down their kiosks. It was the end of the season.

One evening, when they arrived home, Fidget sniffed the air and twitched his whiskers before closing the shop door behind them.

'Jelly me an eel,' he said. 'I think, my little ducks, tonight we'll be moving.'

Now, the idea of the shop having legs and being able to move whenever the wind changed had always worried Emily. In fact, it was her worst nightmare that the shop might up sticks and leave without her. What would she do if she was left all alone? This thought took the sunshine out of the day and she went upstairs to the sitting room while Fidget made tea. She looked out of the window across the road to the beach and a tear rolled down her cheek. She hated things ending.

Emily hadn't noticed Buster sprawled on the sofa. Quickly she dried her eyes. He would only make fun of her if he saw her crying.

Without sitting up, Buster said, 'It's a hatbox thing.'

'What do you mean?' asked Emily.

'You were left as a baby in a hatbox at Stansted Airport and deep inside your head you think it will happen again. But it won't,' said Buster.

'How do you know for sure?'

'Simple,' said Buster. 'I haven't been eleven for a hundred years not to know a thing or two. You are the Keeper of the Keys. You inherited Wings & Co. There is no way the shop would leave you stranded. Don't you understand? It would be lost without you. So I wouldn't worry.'

'Thanks,' said Emily, brightening.

That teatime the magic lamp walked into the kitchen carrying a holdall. Instead of its curly-toed slippers, it had trainers on its feet and round its lid was a sweatband. The lamp was followed by the keys who – if ironmongery can weep – were weeping.

17

'I am staying here in Puddliepool-on-Sea,' said the magic lamp. 'I've explained to Cyril and he is being brave.'

Cyril was the only key not weeping.

'Hold that haddock,' said Fidget. 'What's going on?'

'I have been offered the role I was born to play – the magic lamp in Aladdin! It's my dream come true.'

Emily said, 'But that means . . .'

'It means my career is taking off,' said the magic lamp. 'I don't like goodbyes, but goodbye it is.'

'Well, peel me a prawn,' said Fidget.

'Good riddance,' muttered Buster.

'Oh dear,' said Emily.

'Sweet mistress, forgive me for deserting you, but the bright lights are calling.'

They all trooped up to the shop door and waved goodbye as the magic lamp walked off into the sunset.

'I'll be at the Mermaid Hotel,' it called.

That evening, everyone was a little sad and went to bed early. They were a family, and now one of them had decided to leave, it felt wrong.

Emily wondered how the magic lamp would find them again, if it ever wanted to. She did her best to stay awake, to see for herself the moment when the old shop found its legs but, as with so many magic moments, Emily was fast asleep when it happened.

Next morning they woke to find they were back in Podgy Bottom in the same alley as before, as if they had never been gone. Yet the shop felt a lot quieter, the keys seemed upset, and everyone – even Buster – agreed that they missed the magic lamp.

Buster was flicking through the Podgy Bottom Evening Star when he saw the headline. It read:

MATCHBOX MYSTERIES – WHO SHRUNK THE CARS?

'This,' said Buster, as he read the article, 'has all the signs of fairy mischief.'

How quickly holidays fade, thought Emily. All that happened in Puddliepool-on-Sea belonged to another world. She sighed. Perhaps the magic lamp would send a postcard.

Chapter Three

On the outskirts of Podgy Bottom by the riverbank stood a red-brick Victorian factory. It was one of those tall buildings that had seen grander days, but as time had moved on, became more and more forgotten.

Ben Salisbury was a young businessman. He had rented the old building and started a small business called Scarycrow. It made realistic monsters and other strange electronic toys, all designed by him. The company was doing well; his toys were in great demand. With Hallowe'en round the corner, Ben was often to be found working late at the factory on his latest creation, Scary Chicken Legs. When you put them on, they made you walk like a chicken. They were to be launched as part of Scarycrow's marketing campaign at the Hallowe'en Ball at the Red Lion Hotel.

It was while he was trying out his new invention that Ben first spied a huge purple rabbit sitting in the middle of the factory floor. As far as Ben could remember, he hadn't invented a big purple rabbit. And he certainly hadn't

designed a creature that could eat a lettuce sandwich. So where had it come from? Ben had never seen such a big rabbit. It was enormous – the size of a large dog – and it had the strangest eyes. They spun round in its head and made Ben feel quite giddy.

He closed his own eyes then looked again. The rabbit had vanished. Ben put the worrying vision down to stress and thought nothing more of it. The next time he saw the rabbit, it was standing on a chair examining one of the electronic chicken legs, but the moment Ben tried to catch it, the rabbit escaped.

He asked Jenny from Sales if any of his employees

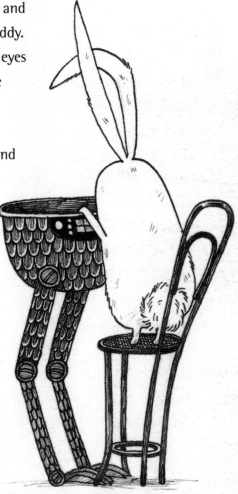

at Scarycrow had seen a purple rabbit. She thought not, though, she added, someone had been taking her lettuce sandwiches.

Ben switched on his computer and typed 'Big Purple Rabbit+Podgy Bottom' into the search engine. He didn't imagine for a moment there would be any results but, bingo, there it was: Purple Rabbit Attacks Farmer. Ben clicked on it. In the village of Bosford, not far from Podgy Bottom, a farmer, Mr Montgomery, aged sixty-three, had been beaten up by a purple rabbit.

'That rabbit had a mighty strong punch,' Mr Montgomery had said. 'I have never been frightened of a rabbit before in my life.' There was a picture of Mr Montgomery covered in bandages. 'I was chased from my own field by that purple rabbit.'

Ben studied the blurry colour photo that the farmer had taken on his mobile phone. Out of focus or in focus, that was the same blooming rabbit that he had seen in his factory. Ben printed out the photo and pinned it on his corkboard.

That evening, he was again working late on the Scary Chicken Legs. They weren't running as smoothly as he would have liked. The movement was still too jerky.

Just as he thought he had corrected the problem he

heard an icy voice say, 'Those are my legs. I want them back.'

Ben looked around and there behind him was the purple rabbit standing on its hind legs.

Ben was flabbergasted. The rabbit had spoken – and spoken very threateningly. He was just thinking that he'd never been threatened by a rabbit before when the rabbit jumped into the air and came straight for him. The punch from that paw was enough to send Ben and the Scary Chicken Legs flying across the factory floor. He landed with a terrible thud and remembered nothing else.

He woke to find his chicken legs gone and two men staring down at him, both wearing balaclavas, one with a pom-pom on top.

'Help – call the police,' said Ben. 'I've been robbed . . .'

'No you haven't. Not yet,' said the man with the pom-pom on top of his balaclava. 'But you are about to be.'

They lifted poor, dazed Ben onto a chair and tied him up. He watched, helpless, as they blew open the safe and took all the petty cash, and went about grabbing as many toys as they could.

After they'd left, Ben spent the rest of the night desperately trying to wiggle free. It was hopeless. The burglars had tied him up good and proper.

He sat there for what felt like a very long time indeed. He thought he saw all sorts of things in the shadows, including a huge rabbit. It appeared to be strapping on the Scary Chicken Legs. It stood up and towered above him before walking away. Ben noted that the movement was a little smoother than before.

Jenny from Sales arrived next morning to hear her boss calling for help. The safe door had been blown open and all the toys were gone. She freed Ben and phoned the police. Sergeant Litton arrived shortly afterwards. He could see that Ben wasn't well. Jenny phoned Ben's friend, Derek Lowe, a landscape gardener, who came to take him home.

'He keeps saying a purple rabbit stole his chicken legs,' Sergeant Litton said. 'Rabbits, as everyone knows, don't come in purple.'

'I'm not bonkers,' said Ben to Derek, as they were driving down Podgy Bottom High Street. 'I did see a purple talking rabbit.'

'Seems to me,' said Derek, 'you need the help of fairy detectives.'

'Do you know any?' asked Ben.

Chapter Four

F idget had a fur ball in his throat. He'd had it ever since they'd come back to Podgy Bottom, which meant, simply, that something wasn't right. Call it animal instinct. Some fairy mischief was afoot, of that he was certain. He had smelled it in the wind before they'd left the seaside and now the smell was even stronger.

Buster thought it might be connected to the car shrinking he'd seen in the paper. He vaguely remembered the case of the Emperor's New Coach, back in 1837. The coach had shrunk, leaving the emperor in an embarrassing situation. Or something like that.

But Fidget felt there was more to this than shrinking cars. Whatever it was, it was beginning to make his fur itch. He couldn't put a paw on the problem until the morning Ben Salisbury walked into Wings & Co.

'You do detective work?' he asked.

'Spot on the fishcake,' said Fidget.

'Even if the case sounds really weird?'

'Especially if it sounds really weird.'

'And you are a . . . ?'

'A cat,' said Fidget.

'OK. Sorry. It's just that I was knocked unconscious by a rabbit and I'm not sure if I'm seeing things . . . like rabbits and . . . er . . . cats. Sounds bonkers, doesn't it?'

'No,' said Fidget. 'It sounds as if you've come to the right place.'

He led Ben up the rickety staircase and, once on the landing, was pleased to see that the sitting room was in exactly the same place it had been a few minutes ago. The shop had a tendency to move rooms about, especially if it didn't like someone. It would even go into lockdown if it wanted to make sure that whoever was in the shop couldn't get out.

Fortunately, today everything was in order, apart from Buster, who was perched on top of the sideboard with his wings outstretched. Emily was curled up with a book in the huge armchair and next to her sat the keys, all in a row. Doughnut lay stretched out beside her.

It was a rather cosy picture, thought Fidget. The only thing missing was a plate of fish-paste sandwiches.

Ben stared open-mouthed at the room. It looked as if it could be out of a museum. Painted dark red with golden stars on the walls, it was stuffed full of books and the strangest of objects. There were pictures everywhere. He was interested to see that the keys each had one leg with a tiny, booted foot that moved of its own accord.

'Wow,' he said.

But it was the wings that really impressed Ben, especially when the boy flew down from the sideboard and folded them away.

'Are they battery-operated?' asked Ben. 'What I would give to have those designs. I mean, they'd sell like hot cakes – and as for the keys, they're well wicked.'

'This,' said Fidget, 'is Ben Salisbury. He was knocked out by a rabbit.'

'And robbed,' added Ben. 'Twice.'

Emily stood up to say hello.

'Oh dear,' she said. 'Once sounds like a misfortune, twice . . .'

'Sounds like a disaster,' said Ben.

'Yes. This is Buster Ignatius Spicer and I'm Emily Vole. We are detectives.'

'But you . . . you're only kids,' stammered Ben.

'I happen to have been eleven for one hundred years,' said Buster. 'Which is, I think, longer than you have been alive.'

'Well – yes,' said Ben.

'Sit down,' said Fidget, sitting himself in his favourite chair and taking up his knitting. He had made considerable progress recently. Before, everything had turned out fish-shaped, but now the coat was coat-shaped and the pattern on it was of fishes.

Ben sat and Doughnut jumped into his lap.

'Don't worry, he's just a dog,' said Emily. 'Unfortunately, none of us are very good at speaking Dog.'

'Wow. This is some place. This is amazing.'

'Now,' said Fidget, 'tell us what's been rocking your fish bowl.'

Ben started with the Scary Chicken Legs, and when he came to the part about the big purple rabbit, Fidget's whiskers twitched.

'Oh no!' said Emily.

Buster was taking notes. He looked up. 'Did you say a purple rabbit?' he asked sharply.

'Yes,' said Ben. 'And it spoke.'

'What did it say?'

'It said, "Those are my legs. I want them back."'

There was a dreadful silence as the three detectives looked at each other.

At last Emily said, 'Was there . . . was there anything else about the bunny that stood out?'

'No. Just that it was big and purple and had a

menacing look in its eye. Oh yeah, it had pink ears. You think I'm bonkers, don't you?'

'Unfortunately, it sounds all too possible,' said Fidget. 'What exactly can those Scary Chicken Legs do?'

'I designed them so they can walk or run depending on which speed you set them on. They were supposed to be the star turn at the Hallowe'en Ball at the Red Lion Hotel.'

'The rabbit didn't have a broomstick, did it?' asked Fidget.

'No,' said Ben.

'Thank my lucky starfish for that,' said Fidget. 'We'll take the case.'

'You will?' said Ben. 'Oh, I nearly forgot. The purple rabbit knocked me out and after that, two men tied me up and stole the petty cash and some toys. Do you think the purple rabbit had anything to do with the second robbery?'

'No,' said Buster. 'Nothing at all. I think the police can deal with that and we'll deal with the rabbit.'

Fidget saw Ben out and waved goodbye. He was about to go back to the sitting room when once more the shop door opened, and there stood a very sad-looking Detective James Cardwell of Scotland Yard.

'Hello, Jimmy, my old sprat. What's up?'

'Can I have a word,' he said, 'in the kitchen?'

'Is this about a rabbit?' asked Fidget.

'No, no. It's more serious.'

'Shrinking cars?'

'No, more serious still.'

'Tell you what. I'll make tea and toast. That always helps, and I'm in need of a fish-paste sandwich or two.'

James sighed.

'It is good to see you,' he said.

The kitchen was in the basement of the shop. The old stove twinkled with coals, pans hung from metal hooks and in a painted sideboard sat all the crotchety crockery arguing as always about what should go where.

'I heard,' said James, 'that the magic lamp stayed behind in Puddliepool-on-Sea.'

'Spot on the fishcake,' replied Fidget. 'It's rehearsing for the role of the magic lamp in Aladdin. Now, tell me – what's up?'

'I'm in love,' said James.

'Well, batter a haddock! That's good, isn't it?'

'No, it's not good,' said James. 'It's hopeless.'

'Why?'

'She's not a fairy. I can't tell her I'm one. It would never work, you know that,' said James miserably.

'What does she do, this lady who's kippered your heart?'

'Poppy's a detective like me. She works at Scotland Yard. In fact, she's my assistant.'

'Emily's not a fairy,' Fidget pointed out. 'And that hasn't stopped her being very understanding.'

'You know why that is. She's one in a million and there's no point in saying otherwise. It's not the same thing.'

Outside the kitchen Buster waited for the subject to change. He had accidentally overheard the whole conversation and he wasn't keen on lovey-dovey stuff. He thought James was being incredibly soppy. As Fidget put the tea and toast on the table, Buster opened the kitchen door.

'Oh, hi, James, great to see you,' he said. 'Fidget, didn't you hear the kerfuffle?'

'No,' said Fidget. 'Don't tell me. A purple rabbit?'

'Come on – one of the keys has just opened a drawer – another fairy has got his wings back.'

'Wait,' said James Cardwell. 'Did you say—'

But Fidget was already halfway up the stairs with Buster. In the shop stood a bewildered-looking gentleman wearing small, round-rimmed glasses. He was trying to balance a tottering pile of books.

'Oh golly gosh,' he said, as he and the books parted company. 'My wings! Oh, by all the happy-ever-afters, I have my wings back. A joyous day indeed. I will wear them with pride and let the other librarians see who I really am.'

'Don't get too carried away,' said James. 'Remember the fairy code. A fairy never forgets it.'

Emily collected the books the librarian had dropped.

'You aren't by chance the famous Emily Vole?' said the librarian.

Emily blushed.

'What an honour, what a day.'

And almost skipping into the air, the librarian flew away over the rooftops of Podgy Bottom, waving goodbye as he went.

'Fidget,' said James, 'did you say purple rabbit a moment ago?'

'I'm afraid so, Jimmy. Harpella the witch is back in town,' said Fidget. 'But there is some good news.'

'What?' said James.

'She hasn't got her broomstick back. Yet.'

Chapter Five

erbie Snivelle's main reason for visiting Podgy
Bottom was to collect his fairy wings. It was with
some regret that he had handed them to Wings & Co.
in the first place. Now that Chicken, as he called his ex-
wife, had been transformed into a purple bunny and her
sidekick, the spirit lamp, had lost its power, there was no
need to stay away. This change in the winds of fortune had
blown Herbie back into town.

Herbie looked at himself in the mirror in his motel
room, adjusted his fedora hat and brushed invisible fluff
from his jacket. The time had come for Wings & Co. to
have a new boss. Time for that cat to hang up his fish
fryer and scoot.

If Fidget had been a bit more understanding in the
first place, thought Herbie, things might have turned out
better. The Fairy Wars weren't Herbie's fault. He'd done
nothing except dump the witch and go into hiding.
No one could blame him; he'd been tricked. Harpella had

put a spell on him – he would never have got hitched to that crazy dame otherwise. He wasn't the marrying kind.

By the time the Fairy Wars were at their height, Herbie had a new squeeze. She wasn't a fairy and Herbie had been very surprised when their baby daughter was born with wings. He'd had no choice but to take them away from her. It was too risky, with his ex-wife and her spirit lamp on the rampage.

He'd parcelled up his daughter's wings with his and left them outside Wings & Co with an unsigned note saying, 'Take care of these wings'.

After that, life had gone disastrously wrong, until he'd pitched up Stateside. But that was all ancient history.

He turned from the mirror to inspect his matchbox collection, all three hundred and sixty-four shrunken cars. There were still a few vehicles he wanted. For a start, he didn't have a builders' white transit van, or one of those impressive black stretch limos that film stars travel about in. But most of all he fancied a big red fire engine.

The sound of a motor scooter made him rush to the window. A blue Vespa jewelled with chrome whizzed past.

I want that, thought Herbie Snivelle. That's a classic must-have. He put his water pistol in its harness and smirked. It was good to be back.

In a lock-up garage in the village of Bosford, the two thieves, Grim and Gravel, were counting the money they had made from last night's factory robbery.

'Not as much as I'd hoped,' said Grim, a wiry man with a shiny bald head and a smile stuck on his face.

Even when he was cross that smile never left him. Gravel was larger, and had Play-Doh features, all soppy and unformed, yet his mind was sharper than an onion knife. He was a very good mechanic and a hopeless burglar.

The Crazy Dinosaur walked across the floor of the garage. Of all the toys they'd stolen from Scarycrow, this was the coolest.

'These toys should make us a tidy sum,' said Grim. 'Any luck working out what that old broomstick's for?'

Gravel put the dinosaur on the workbench next to a broomstick they'd found in a lay-by on the M94. Gravel could see it most definitely wasn't your ordinary household broom, due to the fact that it had a bicycle seat attached to it, and every now and then purple stars would shoot out of its bristles.

He had just finished tightening the bicycle seat so that it wasn't wobbly, when he noticed a small lever underneath it. He pulled it and something extraordinary happened. Rainbow fireworks erupted from the end of the broomstick's bristles and before you could say 'Abracadabra', Gravel found himself clinging on for dear life as the broomstick zoomed round the garage, making a terrible din, bashing into the walls and the garage door.

'That's right,' shouted Grim. 'Let everyone know we're here.'

'I can't stop it,' shouted Gravel.

He could hold on no longer and fell with a thud to the ground. The broomstick came to a shuddering halt and stood upright all by itself.

'Blimey,' said Gravel. 'You don't think it belongs to a witch?'

'Nah,' said Grim. 'Of course it doesn't. They have that other kind of broom, with twigs at the end. This is more your everyday sort of brush. It most probably was a prop from a film set – you know, like Harry Potter. That would explain the pink bristles. It must have fallen off the back of a prop lorry.'

Gravel looked less sure. 'I'm a mechanic and I can tell you this: there are no electrics in that broomstick. So, clever clogs, how does it work?'

The broomstick looked as if it were following the conversation. In fact, it had started to follow Grim round the garage.

'Make it stop,' he said.

'I can't,' said Gravel. 'The thing has a mind of its own.'

Grim looked pale. 'Let's get out of here,' he said.

Together they caught hold of the broomstick. It put up a fight and there was quite a kerfuffle. Finally the crooks managed to shut it in the broom cupboard.

They piled into Gravel's white Ford Transit van. On the side was written:

Grim & Gravel

No Job Too Small or Too Large

As they drove out of the lock-up garage they could hear the broomstick bashing on the broom cupboard door.

'You sure it ain't got electrics in it?' asked Grim, as they pulled away from the garage and onto the open road.

'Certain,' said Gravel.

Chapter Six

It was one of the busiest days at Wings & Co. that Emily had ever known. The keys, usually reluctant to open any of the drawers in the curious cabinets, had had a bonanza and opened one drawer after another. The librarian, two teachers, one accountant and six singers, all from the same chorus, had been brought back to collect their wings.

'I was in the middle of a lesson,' said the maths teacher from Wales. 'I can't just leave my pupils willy-nilly.'

Buster gave him a few flying lessons before he set off rather uncertainly in the direction of his school. The games teacher hadn't lost the knack of flying. She had been keeping very fit and was thrilled to have her wings returned to her but needed to get back to netball practice, pronto. The chorus members were the jolliest of all. They had been friends for ages and each thought the others might be fairies though none had dared say so. Their arrival turned into quite a party. About four o'clock, it broke up and the

sky filled with singers as they flew away towards the Royal Albert Hall.

'Well, marinate a mackerel, what a merry day,' said Fidget. 'Where's Buster?'

'He went up to the roof to see the chorus off,' said Emily.

'Then time for a kip,' said Fidget, making his way to the sitting room.

Emily followed him.

'Can I ask you a question?' she said, as he collapsed into his favourite armchair.

Fidget sniffed and sniffed again.

'What is it?' asked Emily.

'There is something in the wind that is decidedly fishy in the wrong way,' he said. 'If you catch my drift net.'

'Not really,' said Emily. 'Perhaps if I was a fairy I would understand what you're talking about.'

'Oh, don't worry about it,' said Fidget, yawning.

'My question is . . .' said Emily.

Too late. Fidget was purring, fast asleep.

Emily lay on the sofa and had just dozed off, when she and Fidget both woke with a start.

'What's that?' said Emily.

The whole of the shop had started to shudder.

'Buddleia and bindweed!' said Fidget. 'This is what I

suspected all along. Trouble has come our way.'

As Fidget and Emily went downstairs to see who or what was causing the trouble, the shop bell rang. The walls greeted it with a groan.

In the gloomy alleyway stood a man dressed in a pinstripe suit with black-and-white shoes and a fedora hat.

'Bloated barracudas – look what the tide's brought in,' said Fidget.

'That's no way to talk to a long-lost buddy,' said Herbie Snivelle, pushing his way into the shop.

'You're no buddy of mine. You can walk those flashy shoes of yours right out of the door again.'

'I ain't budging without my wings.'

'Your wings?'

'Yeah, I left them here for safekeeping. With my kid's.'

Fidget's fur stood on end, making him look enormous. He was furious.

'You don't get anything, you rotten, stinking shark.'

'No need to be rude. Just gimme my wings.'

'It's not that easy,' said Emily.

'Who's the kid?' said Herbie.

'This is Emily Vole,' said Fidget. 'She's the Keeper of the Keys now.'

'Great. Get those keys to open my drawer, baby, and hand me my wings toot sweet.'

'It doesn't work like that. The keys only open drawers if the mood takes them.'

'Then you're the keeper of nothing,' said Herbie. 'Quit wasting my time. Hand over that miserable bunch of ironmongery and let me put them straight. Now. Or I'll get angry. And when Herbie Snivelle gets angry—'

'You can't bully Emily. Leave this minute,' said Fidget.

Herbie went up to Fidget and put his face very close to the cat's.

'Listen to me, you flea-ridden old has-been. Get outta town.'

It was then that the shop stood up on its stout iron legs and shook itself, like a dog ridding itself of a flea. Emily and Fidget managed to cling to the counter by a whisker as the shop tilted at such an angle that Herbie Snivelle tumbled out of the door and landed with a terrible bump on the pavement below. The shop righted itself again with a sigh of relief, leaving Emily and Fidget rather dazed. They peered out. They were as high as the roof tops and Herbie Snivelle was below, shaking his fist at them.

'You'll regret this, you mangy cat. No one messes with Herbie, no one. Lemme tell you this: like it or not, Wings & Co is gonna have a new boss. Start packing if you know what's good for you.'

Fidget closed the door.

'I had a feeling when the wind changed that a whole load of stale seaweed was drifting our way,' he said.

'Who is he?' asked Emily.

'He, my little ducks, is one of the nastiest fairies you're ever likely to meet. That squirt with shark's teeth was responsible for the Fairy Wars. And I can tell you this for a barrelful of herring: he is bad news all the way down to the last rotten prawn.'

'Oh – you mean he's the fairy who married Harpella then ditched her? What are we going to do?'

'It's a good question, and one I don't have the answer to. But I have a feeling that Harpella knows Herbie's back. And bunny or no bunny, a witch never forgets. Or forgives.'

Chapter Seven

Karen Pin's dress shop was opposite the bank in Podgy Bottom High Street. Karen's mother, Maureen, who was newly widowed, was sitting by the counter with Hellman, her small, yapping Jack Russell terrier. He started howling when a very odd-looking creature tottered in.

'Karen,' shouted Maureen to her daughter, 'you have a customer. A purple bunny with chicken legs.'

'Mum, stop it! How many times have I told you not to be rude about the customers?' said Karen, as she came into the shop from the storeroom.

The moment she saw the creature she was lost for words.

'It looks bad, I know,' said Harpella in a voice like gravel on ice. 'I've had a slight accident but I'm recovering slowly.'

'How can I help?' said Karen shakily.

'I need a cocktail dress – nothing that will clash with

purple, you understand. Maybe in turquoise . . . or that,' she said, pointing at an electric orange frock.

'You'll look like the dog's dinner,' said Maureen Pin, while Hellman continued to yap.

'Does that dog – or your mother – ever stop yapping?' asked Harpella.

'No. Unfortunately,' said Karen. 'She's a bit deaf and, well, since Dad died she's been living with me.'

'Why?' said Harpella.

'She's lonely. I gave her the dog to keep her quiet and all the dog does is bark. What size?' said Karen.

'Small,' said Harpella.

'You're sure black wouldn't look better?'

'No,' said Harpella. 'I wouldn't want anyone thinking I'm a witch.'

She took the cocktail dress and went into the changing room.

'You shouldn't be seen serving a purple rabbit with chicken legs,' said Maureen. 'It's not good for business.'

'Please, Mum,' whispered Karen. 'She's a customer.'

'I'll take it,' said Harpella, drawing back the curtain dramatically. She looked at herself in the mirror from all angles.

Karen's mouth fell open.

Before her was a terrifying sight. A purple rabbit's head

stuck out of the orange dress, the sleeves of which were a mile too long and flapped about. A lime-green scarf was tied wildly round the rabbit's pink ears in a failed attempt to hide them. That was not the strangest thing. The body shape was completely disjointed, sticking out at the oddest angles. Karen couldn't work out whether she was more frightening with or without the dress. And no shoes could hide those chicken feet.

'All you need is a broomstick and you'll be made, woman,' said Maureen.

'When I have mine back,' said Harpella, 'you'd better watch out.'

'Well, I never!' said Maureen. 'Are you threatening me?'

Fortunately, Harpella wasn't listening, for if she had been it wouldn't have ended well. Her attention was caught by the sight of the young man from the electronic toy factory.

Without her broomstick, Harpella couldn't do a lot about being a bunny, but a plan was beginning to form. Throwing some cash on the counter, she left the shop and followed Ben down the road.

'Cooeee,' she called.

Ben turned and let out a small scream.

'You're the rabbit I saw in my factory,' he said.

'That's so clever of you,' said Harpella. 'And I'm wearing your chicken legs – look.'

'What do you want from me?' said Ben, backing away.

'I want you to make me into a new woman,' said Harpella.

'Leave me alone,' said Ben. He started to walk faster then broke into a run, but however fast he went, Harpella was at his heels.

'You see,' she said, 'you designed the chicken legs very well.'

'Leave me alone,' said Ben again. 'I don't know who you are, but leave me alone.'

Suddenly she was in front of him, blocking his way. He stared into large, soft bunny eyes that appeared to whirl round and round in the rabbit's head. Try as he might, he couldn't look away, and he felt himself to be disappearing into the whirlpools until at last his mind was completely clear. All he knew was that he would obey the purple bunny with chicken legs.

'That's better,' said Harpella. 'Now, find a taxi and let's get to work.'

Harpella, without the Scary Chicken Legs, sat on the floor of the factory looking at the drawings of the new woman she was about to become. According to her wishes, it was to have a womanly shape, working arms and hands with red steel fingernails, and faster-running chicken legs. It had to be comfortable for a rabbit to sit in and control by only a paw. Ben had been working on a prototype robot that hadn't quite taken shape and he was adapting the design to Harpella's desires.

Like everyone else in the factory, Jenny was somewhat worried by the change in Ben's behaviour. He looked as if he was sleep-walking and instead of the sweet, easy-going boss they all knew, he had become bad-tempered and obsessed with making the body to go with the chicken legs. Ben's assistant had tried to find out what was up, but one glare from Ben stopped anyone else from asking questions. They just had to trust that he knew what he was doing. After all, he'd never let them down before.

After three days, the prototype was ready to be tested. When Ben tried to help Harpella into the control seat, she froze.

'Don't touch me,' she spat at him, and hopped in unaided. Ben stood back as she began to walk about.

'Very good. Very good indeed,' she said.

Just then, Jenny from Sales came in with a coffee and a bun for Ben. When she saw the half-woman, half-bird robot with a purple rabbit's head and pink ears, she let out a terrible scream and dropped the tray.

'What's that?'

'The new toy,' said Ben.

'It's gross,' said Jenny, picking up pieces of crockery.

'It's only a prototype,' said Ben.

'Then it needs a proper human face. That bunny thing just isn't working.'

Just as Jenny had gathered all the bits of china, the bunny spoke.

'She has a point,' said Harpella. 'I need my face back.'

Chapter Eight

It was the most serious situation Wings & Co had ever found themselves in. Herbie Snivelle wasn't leaving – far from it. He'd been back several times, threatening to smash the windows, break down the door and throw the fairy detectives into the street. He meant every word of what he said. He wanted his wings back, he wanted Fidget out of the shop and he wanted to run the joint himself.

The very thought of Herbie Snivelle coming anywhere near the curious cabinets made the floors rock, the walls shudder and the window panes rattle. Emily, Fidget and Buster felt as if they were adrift on a stormy sea.

Fidget called the solicitor, Mr Alfred Twizzell, for advice. He was a fairy and knew all about fairy ways. He had dealt with the estate of their dear friend, the late Miss String.

'Oh dear, oh dear,' he said, on hearing that Herbie Snivelle was back. 'I'm most terribly afraid that if that is the case, Harpella won't be far behind, bunnified or not.'

'There have been sightings of a purple bunny in the neighbourhood,' said Fidget.

'Please tell me she doesn't have the broomstick,' said Alfred Twizzell.

'We don't think so, dear old cod,' said Fidget.

'Even so, I needn't tell you that Emily is not safe,' said Alfred Twizzell. 'Neither, for that matter, are you or Buster, and especially not the keys. My advice is that you pack up and leave the shop straight away. Move into a hotel, at least for the time being, then the shop will be able to take the standard security measures and board itself up. It's the only way to make sure no unwanted witches or their ex-husbands can enter.'

'We can't go on like this, being jiggled and joggled from morning to night,' said Emily, as Fidget hung up and the shop had another bout of the heebie-jeebies. 'It's been nearly two days now.'

'I feel seasick,' said Buster. He looked more than a little green about the gills. 'Have you seen the paper?' He waved it at Emily. 'I'm too ill to read it. Something about three more burglaries.'

Emily read the article out loud.

'"Miss Karen Pin, the shop owner, was held up at bristle point by a broomstick until two thieves made their escape

with the day's takings." How can a broomstick hold up a
shop?' asked Emily.

'Read that again,' said Buster and Fidget together.

'Buddleia,' said Fidget when Emily had finished. 'That's
all we need.'

'Will you please explain what or who this broomstick
is?' said Emily. 'And don't tell me I won't understand
because I'm a human.'

Buster groaned. 'I wouldn't dream of it,' he said.
'Fidget, you explain. I feel too sick.'

'You remember, little ducks, when you and the magic
lamp shot Harpella out of the air and turned her into a
purple bunny?' said Fidget.

'How could I forget?' said Emily.

'Well, do you remember what she was riding at the
time?'

'Of course. She was on her . . . oh! Her broomstick.
And you think this broomstick that's robbed Miss Pin
is . . . ?'

'Harpella's broomstick. It's very powerful, and if
Harpella finds it before we do, she will be able to change
herself back into the witch she always was.'

'In that case,' said Emily, 'we can't just sit here being
rolled around. We must find the broomstick. And what
about Ben? It's impossible to investigate anything with the

shop behaving like this and Herbie Snivelle on the loose.'

'And I don't know how much more of this see-sawing I can take,' said Buster from the depths of the sofa, as the floor began to roll one way, then the other. 'I can't think straight or see straight. Will someone fetch me a bucket?'

A picture fell off the wall.

'Oh, not again,' said Emily. 'Do you think they have pictures in boats?' she asked, trying to put it back.

'No,' said Buster. 'If they did they would always be falling to the floor. I really do need a bucket. I think I'm going to be sick.'

'Time to leave, shipmates,' said Fidget. 'Emily is right. We can't stay here when there's work to be done.'

In no time at all, Fidget, Buster, Emily and Doughnut were standing forlornly outside the shop, each with a small suitcase. They watched as the shop swiftly boarded itself up. It looked quite abandoned.

'It's so sad to see the old place like this,' said Emily. 'It's a shop without a smile.'

'It's for the best,' said Fidget. 'You have the keys, my little ducks?'

'Yes,' said Emily. 'They are safe in my suitcase. I counted them once, twice and then once again for luck.'

'Spot on the fishcake. Come along,' said Fidget.

'Where are we going?' asked Buster, who was regaining

his land legs and feeling a little better.

'To the Red Lion Hotel,' said Fidget.

'But they don't take animals and we have Doughnut,' said Emily.

'I think they just might make an exception this once. Remember, if it wasn't for us Joan and the manager would still be bunnified.'

Joan the receptionist was very pleased to see them.

'Oh, Mr Fidget,' she said. 'Welcome back to the Red Lion. Still wearing the same cat suit I see.'

'Yes,' said Fidget. 'And I still have the same medical condition. But this time we do have a small dog.'

'Oh dear,' said Joan, her smile crumbling. 'You know we don't allow pets.'

'I do,' said Fidget. 'May I speak to Mr Flower please?'

Joan picked up the phone and muttered into it.

'He'll be here in a mo,' she said, her nose twitching.

They waited until Mr Flower, the manager, hop-skipped into the lobby.

'Mr Fidget! A pleasure to see you again, sir. And Miss Vole – and a young gentleman. Delightful. What can I do to help?'

'I could put them in the Atlantic Suite,' said Joan, 'but they have a small dog.'

Mr Flower looked down at the longhaired miniature dachshund. Doughnut was wearing one of Fidget's fish knits and his head stuck out of the fish's mouth.

'No, no, no, Joan. Remember we do allow fish and that is a piranha on a lead.'

'Spot on the fishcake. It has the nature of a sea bass without the salt,' said Fidget.

'Quite,' said the manager.

He showed them to the lift and took them to the third floor where he opened up the Atlantic Suite for them.

'You have here,' he said with pride, 'our finest set of rooms. The sitting room boasts a real log-effect fire and widescreen TV. There are four bedrooms, all with balconies and en-suite bathrooms. There is, of course, Wi-Fi. Should you need anything else, please don't hesitate to ask Joan.'

Once he had gone, Fidget sat down in one of the soft armchairs.

'I think,' he said, 'it's room service for us and fish and chips all round.'

Later that afternoon, a parcel arrived for Emily, very badly wrapped with lots of sticky tape. It must have been by a bit of magic that it found Emily because it was addressed to her at Wings & Co.

'What is it?' asked Buster, looking up from his laptop. There had been another broomstick robbery.

'Search my catnip,' said Fidget. 'I can see in the dark but I can't see through brown paper.'

Emily tried to open the parcel, but it was hopeless without scissors. Fidget used his claws but still none of the sticky tape would budge.

'Oh, forget it. We'll have to call Joan and ask for scissors,' said Buster. 'Look, there's an e-fit of the broomstick online. See? It has a saddle and pink bristles. Doesn't that sound like Harpella's broomstick to you?'

Fidget stared at the screen.

'So – we have Herbie Snivelle, a broomstick with pink bristles, two robbers and one purple bunny with chicken legs. Plus Ben from the Scarycrow factory.'

Emily was on the phone to Joan when the parcel jumped off the table.

'Buddleia – what's in there?' said Buster.

'Oh Joan, please be quick with the scissors,' said Emily. 'We have a bit of an emergency.'

The parcel rolled around the floor with Doughnut chasing after it, barking furiously. Then, from under the layers of brown paper came a pitiful voice.

'Sweet mistress – help me!'

Chapter Nine

E ven with Joan's scissors it took a while to unwrap
the parcel. When at last they did, there stood a
woebegone magic lamp. Emily was thrilled to see it again,
but somehow the magic lamp looked different. Its arms,
which had always been skinny, were now so pumped full
of muscle that they stuck out at the sides, and as for its
golden tummy, it seemed to have shrunk at the bottom
and expanded at the top. Its lid had become the size of a
peanut. It definitely didn't look its old self.

'Oh, my sweet mistress,' said the lamp, throwing its
arms round Emily's ankles. 'I have missed you.'

'Me too,' said Emily, picking up the lamp and giving it
a squeeze.

The keys, who were all sitting in a row on the sofa,
didn't budge.

'I'm home,' shouted the magic lamp, its arms wide
open to greet them, but the keys didn't seem that pleased
to see it. Cyril even turned away.

'Oh, Cyril, not you!' cried the magic lamp. 'Is this any way to welcome home someone who has been humiliated? Yes, humiliated, I tell you! I, the greatest magic lamp ever, who was going to star in Aladdin.'

'Usually,' said Emily, 'the magic lamp doesn't have much of a part.'

'You can say that again,' said the magic lamp. 'But I expected to break the mould. I had even been promised lines. Instead, that fat lungfish of an actor who played the genie threw me about the place as if I was a piece of old junk. Humiliated, that's what I was.'

'Lungfish?' said Fidget. 'Oh dear.'

'I was gagged,' continued the magic lamp. 'Mine was a silent part. And after all the preparation I had put into the role . . . the personal trainer, the weights, the dumb bells, press ups, running machines . . . and that was before a good rub down and polish. Yet for all my shape changing and shine dedication, I wasn't allowed into the Green Room with the other actors because I was seen as a prop! A PROP, I TELL YOU! At the end of the day's rehearsal I was left on the stage manager's desk. I had to climb down from a terrible height, night after night, to get back to my hotel. Finally, I had it out with the director. I told him I would not be treated like that. I was vital to the plot and I needed my own dressing room. Do you know what he told me? That any old lamp would do and I was the wrong shape. Me! How could he tell ME I was the wrong shape? Humiliated, I was, and not a friend in the world. Then one day the stage manager grabbed hold of me without so much as a please or a thank you or a by your leave and smothered me in masses and masses of brown paper. I shouted, "I am not to be treated like this!" I called for help. I screamed. All to no avail. Humiliated. What more can I say?'

'Swipe me with a kipper,' said Fidget. 'If you said any more, we would have to give you a standing ovation.'

'What does that mean?' asked Emily, passing the magic lamp a box of tissues.

'It's what they do in a theatre when an actor has given a moving speech. They give him an extra round of applause.'

'Oh, sweet mistress, I knew only you would understand my pain,' said the magic lamp. He blew his spout as tears rolled down his golden belly. 'I have been abused, used and bruised. My pride has taken a terrible tumble. I phoned my agent to complain and he said the role of the lamp was limited and that really it was the genie that mattered. The genie! I have suffered very badly. The theatre is not all it's cracked up to be.'

The keys climbed off the bed and surrounded the magic lamp as if to say he was forgiven for leaving them.

'Well, you're back now, my old fish bait,' said Fidget. 'And not a moment too soon. We need you.'

'You do?' sniffed the magic lamp.

'Yes,' said Emily.

'Yes,' mumbled Buster.

'How so?' asked the magic lamp, cheering up a little.

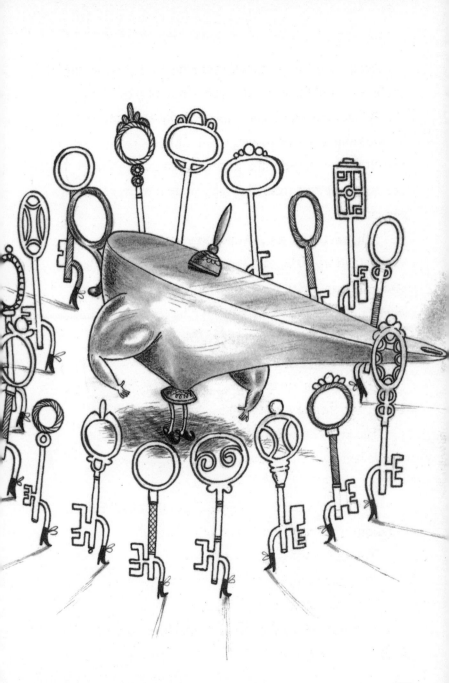

Buster told him all that had happened and about the broomstick robberies.

'Oh no,' said the magic lamp. 'You're not talking about a broomstick with pink bristles and a bicycle seat on its handle?'

'Yes,' said Emily, showing it the e-fit. 'Do you recognise it?'

'Of course I do. I had to live with that bullying broomstick when I was Harpella's prisoner. I tell you, sweet mistress, I wouldn't trust it with a tea tray. Even the old witch kept it in a broom cupboard. She had to – why, the thing was so moody. Oh yippee! I can see I haven't come home a day too soon.'

Chapter Ten

etective James Cardwell was called into the
Detective Chief Inspector's office and asked to lead
the investigation into what were to be codenamed the
Matchbox Mysteries.

'This is top-secret stuff,' said the DCI. 'Cars are being
shrunk to matchbox size before their owners' eyes. We have
some reliable witnesses in London and also in Bishop's
Stortford. What's going on, Cardwell?' He handed James a
thick folder. 'The most recent report is from Podgy Bottom.
I believe you know the area?'

'Yes, sir. I investigated the death of Sir Walter Cross.'

James vaguely remembered Fidget mentioning
shrinking cars when he had flown to Podgy Bottom to ask
his advice. He now regretted that he hadn't taken more
notice. But his mind had been on other things – like Poppy.
In fact it was hard to think of anything else except Poppy.

'I'm sending Detective Poppy Perkins with you,' said the
DCI. 'She'll assist with the investigation.'

James felt a moment of panic. His wings started to flutter under his jacket.

'I would rather go on my own, sir. I don't need anyone to assist me.'

'Cardwell, Detective Perkins is an expert in solving cases of ah – let's say – an unusual nature. I worked with her years ago when I was a young detective.' He laughed. 'She's like you – never seems to age. In fact, she doesn't look a day older than when I first met her.'

'When was that?' said James.

'Not important, Cardwell. What's important is that you get to the bottom of this shrinking car business. The Home Secretary is on my back. I want results and I want them fast.'

James picked up the file and went up to his office.

This is becoming unworkable, he thought. If only I could tell Poppy how I feel about her. And that I'm a fairy. Maybe I should ask for a transfer. It's not doing me any good being around her. In fact, it's making me miserable.

Just then he received a curious text from Fidget.

spot of trouble. shop in lockdown.

moved to red lion hotel.

What's that all about? James wondered, as he unlocked his private filing cabinet where he kept his records of fairy mischief. He was certain the Matchbox Mysteries were a case of fairy meddling, the sort of thing he was well used to. But which fairy? There had been quite a few fairies with the habit of shrinking things. They'd caused no end of trouble over the years.

His mobile phone announced another text. Fidget again.

4got to say. herbie snivelle back.

Herbie Snivelle. A nasty piece of work. Capable of anything. Detective Cardwell pulled out some dusty-looking files and flicked through them until he found what he was looking for.

During the Fairy Wars, Herbie Snivelle went into hiding. It is understood that he met a human, an actress called Milly Turtle, and had a child with her. Herbie deserted mother and baby and in 1776 was reported to have sailed to America. Milly Turtle died in London in 1790. The child's fate is unknown.

Nothing about shrinking.

'Buddleia,' he said out loud.

'Can I help?'

He spun round to see Poppy standing in the doorway, as pretty as a picture, her blonde bob gleaming.

'Thank you, Poppy, it's nothing. I'm just mumbling to myself,' said James, going bright red.

'I'm ready to go whenever you are, Guv,' said Poppy.

James hadn't thought that they would travel to Podgy Bottom together. Truth be told, he was rather looking forward to spreading his wings and flying. He needed time alone to think and clear his head. This nonsense had to stop.

'Shall I get a car from the car pool?' she asked helpfully.

It was then James remembered that years ago he had put one of his favourite cars in a garage for safe-keeping. He had the keys somewhere.

'No,' he said, frantically searching his desk drawer. At last he found the key. 'I'll drive if you don't mind taking a spin with an old wreck – I mean, in an old wreck.'

'Not at all,' said Poppy. 'It'll be fun.'

The old wreck, as James called it, was a 1957 Austin Healey, as spanking new as a car that age could be. It was shiny red with a cream soft-top and looked very stylish indeed.

'Wow,' said Poppy. 'If I had a car like this I wouldn't just keep it in a garage. I would be out in it all the time. And I love tinkering with engines.'

'I'm hopeless. I don't know a petrol tank from a fish tank,' said James, trying to keep his eyes on the road.

They were going over a small hill, the kind of hill that makes you think you have left your tummy behind, when it came to Detective Cardwell, somewhat belatedly, that Herbie could be the reason a certain purple rabbit had been sighted near Podgy Bottom. Why had he been so slow to work it out? There wasn't a moment to lose. Fidget, Emily, Buster and the keys were in great danger. He put his foot on the accelerator – and the car came to a grinding halt.

'Don't worry, Guv,' said Poppy. She slid out of the car and lifted up the bonnet. 'I'll have it fixed in no time.'

James looked admiringly at Poppy, and longingly down the road. And wished he had flown.

Chapter Eleven

ow that the lamp was back in the bosom of the family, Emily felt that they could start doing what Wings & Co was supposed to be doing – detective work. They had on their plate perhaps one of their most serious cases yet, and their fear of Harpella and Herbie Snivelle had held everything up.

The time had come to examine the scene of the crime. The next morning, Emily put on her satchel which held her notebook and coloured pens, Fidget put on his hat and fish scarf, and Buster put on his coat to hide his wings. Just before they left, Fidget disappeared and came back with an old-fashioned box camera.

'It's all we have to take photos with and the thing has never let us down,' he said.

'What do you have to do?' asked Emily, taking the camera and turning it upside down.

'It's really very simple,' said Fidget.

'Just say "Click",' said the box camera.

Emily nearly dropped it but said, 'Click,' without thinking what she was clicking at.

'Now,' said Fidget, 'when you're ready, say "Print".'

Emily did, and from the bottom of the camera fell a picture of Emily's right nostril.

'Works every time,' said Fidget. 'Much better than those new-fangled contraptions.'

The magic lamp, after a lot of ooing and umming, decided to stay behind with the keys and Doughnut. It was exhausted after its travels and needed to rest.

'Anyway, I don't think my constitution could put up with much more drama,' it said.

'That would be a first,' said Fidget through his whiskers.

'I heard that,' said the lamp. 'And I would like to state here and now: there are two ways for a magic lamp to go. One is to be nothing more than a selfless vessel for a genie, the other is to stand up and say, 1 matter. And 1 do – 1 matter a great deal!'

The keys all jumped up and down and the magic lamp bowed.

'Oh, let's go before we have to sit through another performance,' said Buster.

The three of them caught the bus from the stop by the statue of Queen Victoria in the town square. The bus driver studied Fidget as he counted out the fare.

'Excuse me for asking, but do you ever take off that cat costume?'

'It's a medical condition,' said Fidget.

'Oh,' said the bus driver. 'Sorry, mate.'

'1 have a bad feeling about this,' said Fidget, as they sat down. 'We've kept Ben hanging on a fishing line for too long.'

'I'm sure it'll be all right,' said Emily, though she was not at all sure it would be all right and felt that most probably it would be all wrong.

'1 hope so, my little ducks,' said Fidget. 'But 1 smell something rotten in the town of Podgy Bottom.'

The bus stopped quite close to the Scarycrow factory. They were met by Jenny from Sales, who looked very worried indeed. She told them that Ben had locked himself in his workshop and hadn't been seen since he'd demonstrated the prototype of the robot.

'What robot?' asked Buster.

This was definitely not sounding good.

'It's a strange-looking thing,' said Jenny from Sales. 'When I saw it, it had a purple rabbit head with pink bunny ears. It gave me the heebie-jeebies. I told Ben it was too scary so he's making it a face. It'll be the scariest of all the toys he has ever designed – it will go down a storm at the Hallowe'en Ball.'

'Did the robot, by any chance, have chicken legs?' asked Fidget.

'Yes,' said Jenny. 'With chicken feet.'

'And Ben hasn't come out at all?' said Fidget. 'Not even to eat?'

'Not once. In fact, he really hasn't been himself since he started on the robot. We put his food outside the cat-flap in the door. He takes in the tray and when it's empty he leaves it outside. Apart from that he might as well be a ghost. Should we be worried?' she asked.

Emily wanted to say, 'Yes, you should be very worried. You should have been very worried days ago.' But she didn't.

The workroom where Ben was holed up was well and truly locked, except for the large cat-flap. A plate and a mug had been left outside it. Emily moved them, lay flat on her tummy and quietly opened the cat-flap. Ben was sitting forlornly on a chair looking as if he was awake and asleep at the same time. She could just see, in the corner of the room, a metal, headless robot in an orange dress. What Emily took to be the head of the robot sat on the workbench – as did a large purple bunny rabbit. Taking out the little camera, Emily started to photograph the scene. When she'd finished she leapt to her feet.

'Print,' she said.

'Well?' asked Fidget.

'It's bad,' whispered Emily, as the camera spewed out the photos. Buster and Fidget studied them. The purple rabbit was unmistakeable.

'Oh, buddleia,' said Buster.

'Oh, buddleia indeed,' said Fidget, looking over his shoulder.

'I don't understand,' said Emily. 'I thought you said Harpella would stay a harmless bunny rabbit for hundreds of years.'

'But that's the thing with witches,' said Buster. 'Their job is breaking spells as well as making them.'

'If she were to find her broomstick, we really would be in a bucketful of eels,' said Fidget.

'Well, we can't just stand here and do nothing,' said Buster. He lay down on the floor and started to squeeze himself through the cat-flap.

'Buster!' said Emily. 'What if she changes you into a rabbit again?'

'Someone,' said Buster nobly, 'has to save Ben.'

Fidget and Emily waited. From inside the workroom they could hear screeching followed by bumps and thumps. Suddenly the door burst open and Buster emerged through a haze of pink smoke leading a very dazed Ben.

Buster slammed the workshop door behind them. 'Quick,' he said. 'Let's get out of here.'

Just then the large purple rabbit stuck its head through the cat-flap. In a voice that could freeze sandpaper, she said,

'You will regret this for ever

and ever

and ever

and ever.'

Chapter Twelve

Grim and Gravel had never in all their years of
burgling imagined that they would end up being
bossed and bullied by a household broom. But
that's exactly what had happened. To their amazement the
broomstick had sprouted arms with leather-gloved hands.
On its bicycle saddle, it wore round, horn-rimmed glasses.
If a broomstick could look menacing, this one did.

For the first time ever Grim and Gravel slept at night
on mattresses full of money. They had never been as
successful at the burgling business as they had been since
the broomstick's arrival. It had swept them into the ranks
of master criminals – which should have made them fond
of the broomstick. But here's the rub: the two crooks
hated to admit, even to each other, that they were scared
rotten of it. In fact, they hardly dared move, let alone
speak, when the broomstick was present, for if they did, it
was likely to go on the attack and thwack them with its
bristles. Grim was rather bruised, Gravel rather battered, and

both were very unhappy. They had begun to plot how they might get rid of the broomstick but it was proving a much bigger problem than either of them thought. For a start it was so blooming clever. It seemed to know what they were thinking before they knew what they were thinking themselves, which made coming up with a plan to outsmart it nearly impossible.

Grim and Gravel stood with their backs against the garage door, trying to keep their minds blank while the broomstick studied an ancient map of Podgy Bottom and the plans of Podgy Bottom's bank. The minute an idea came to it, sparks flew from its bristles and it snapped its fingers. This meant Grim and Gravel were needed. They stood nervously either side of the broomstick while with a pencil it pointed on the old map to where Miss Pin's dress shop now stood.

'I don't get it,' said Gravel. 'We done Miss Pin's only the other day.'

The broomstick whacked him over the head.

'Whoa – what's that for?'

The broomstick jabbed its pencil at the map then started to sharpen it. Sharpening 2B pencils was a habit of the broomstick's; it got through five packets of pencils a day and swept up the shavings as it went.

With the sharpened pencil in its leather-gloved hand it

pointed once more to the site of Miss Pin's shop. A dotted line showed a tunnel which ran under the street to the building opposite.

'That's the bank,' said Gravel.

The broomstick, which was really quite a talented artist, drew a comic strip of what it had in mind.

Grim was to break into Miss Pin's shop late at night, find the entrance to the tunnel and go through into the bank vaults. The opening of the safe was to be left to the broomstick. Gravel was to wait outside in the white transit van and help to fill it with the bags of dosh.

It looked easy enough.

'When?' asked Grim.

The broomstick drew a round moon.

'Full moon,' said Gravel. 'Tomorrow night, then.'

The broomstick pointed to Gravel, then to the drawing of the van.

'All right,' said Gravel. 'I'll fill it up and check the oil and petrol.'

Grim went to leave with him, but the broomstick brushed him back. Ever since it had taken over, they hadn't been allowed to do anything together. Grim watched silently as Gravel took the van keys and went out.

The white van was parked in a side street away from the garage. Gravel was proud of the van. Van and man had been together for years. It wasn't the most modern model, more . . . vintage, a collector's piece. He'd just lifted the bonnet to check the oil when he heard someone come whistling up the road.

'That's a beaut,' said an American voice.

Gravel hit his head on the bonnet as he straightened up.

'I've always wanted one like that,' said the stranger. 'Are you Gravel?' Gravel looked about him shiftily.

'How do you know my name?'

'It's on the side of your van. '"No job too small or too large". Personally, I like small.'

He held out his hand. Gravel found he was staring at an odd-looking man dressed as a gangster. He had a mean look to him. Gravel thought he looked like Al Capone and for a moment wondered if he would be able to stand up to the broomstick. He couldn't see this gangster being bullied by a load of bristles.

'What do you use it for?' asked Herbie Snivelle.

Gravel shrugged. 'Oh, y'know, this and that.'

At that moment a police car drove past. The one thing Gravel couldn't stand was police cars. They made him nervous.

'Nice to meet you,' he said, 'but I have to go.' Without thinking he added, 'Do you want a lift?'

'Sure,' said Herbie Snivelle, and got into the passenger seat.

Gravel slid into the driver's seat and crunched the gears as he turned the van round and headed to the nearest petrol station.

Herbie couldn't believe his luck. Rarely did he have a chance to ride in a vehicle he was about to shrink. When they arrived at the petrol station, Gravel filled the tank and went inside to pay. Through the window he saw Herbie Snivelle get out of the van. Gravel had just helped himself to three chocolate bars, when he stopped. Herbie took out a huge water pistol and fired it at the van. What was he up to? Gravel's mouth fell open and he watched in horror as his beloved white van began to shrink.

'Yes?' said the girl behind the till. 'Which pump?'

Gravel could hardly find the words.

Herbie Snivelle was picking up a tiny white van from the forecourt.

'Which pump number?' said the girl.

Herbie Snivelle was putting it in a matchbox and walking away.

'Pump Three,' said Gravel faintly.

The girl at the till looked out of the window at Pump Three.

'There's nothing there,' she said.

Chapter Thirteen

Harpella had a problem. Now that Ben had been taken by the wretched Buster Ignatius Spicer, who was going to put her new head on? There was no time to lose. Once the smoke had cleared, all those people who worked for Ben would be in the workshop trying to stop her from taking the robot. She made a desperate leap from the workbench into the robot body and settled herself in position. It was a matter of working it from the inside.

Someone outside the door said, 'I think we should call the police.'

With great difficulty, Harpella used the robot's steel hands to pick up the head. The trouble was that she couldn't see what she was doing and she ended up putting it on backwards.

It was like this that she made her escape past Scarycrow's employees, who were all too terrified to stop her. She was, without doubt, the most terrifying electric-orange cocktail-dressed robot ever let loose.

There were sightings of her throughout the day. Sergeant Litton had never known the police station phones to ring so often. Even his mother called to say she had seen a robot in her garden. It had taken a designer scarf off her washing line.

'And Dumpty,' she added, 'you'd better get it back otherwise Mumsy will be very cross indeed with her little boy.'

It was as Harpella tottered along the High Street that she spotted a poster in the window of Martin's, Podgy Bottom's department store.

**Come inside and be transformed by Mrs Scarlatti,
make-up artist to the stars.**

To the stars, read Harpella. Then she is the make-up
artist for me.

That morning, Mrs Scarlatti had forgotten to put in
her contact lenses, a terrible mistake. Already one lady
had complained to the management of the shop that Mrs
Scarlatti had made her look like a witch.

'I know it's Hallowe'en the day after tomorrow,' said
the disgruntled customer, 'but really, this isn't funny.'

Mrs Scarlatti had been told she must do better or be
sacked. It was with a sense of great relief that she saw a
bald lady in an orange dress coming towards her. Here was
a chance to prove what she could do.

'Madam,' said Mrs Scarlatti. 'Let me transform you.'

Harpella caught a glimpse of herself in the mirror.
Her head was on backwards. It struck the witch that was
perhaps the reason so many people had been staring at
her.

'First of all,' said Harpella, 'help me turn my head
round.'

'Of course, madam,' said Mrs Scarlatti, giving it a twist.
'Are you suffering from a stiff neck?'

To Mrs Scarlatti's blurred vision it did make the lady

look a little better, though she had to admit this was a challenge if ever there was one.

'This isn't going to take all day, is it?' hissed Harpella. Already a crowd had gathered to watch.

'I think, madam,' said Mrs Scarlatti, 'we should start with a wig.'

'As long as it's purple,' said Harpella, 'I don't mind.'

'Madam, you have a very colourful style, if I may say so.'

'Stop babbling and get on with it,' said Harpella.

An hour later the transformation was complete. Wearing a purple wig, false eyelashes and bright red lipstick, Harpella was ready to face the world.

The watching crowd clapped. And as Harpella left, Mrs Scarlatti was surprised to find herself mobbed by children all wanting to be made up as witches.

Chapter Fourteen

en sat in an armchair in Wings & Co's suite at the Red Lion Hotel. He was paler than a lemon sorbet and, rather alarmingly, his eyes were going round and round in his head. They made Emily feel dizzy.

'Do you think we should call a doctor?' she asked.

'No,' said Buster. 'It will pass. Anyway, how would we explain to a doctor what's happened to him? Best he sleeps it off.'

'Is that possible?' said Emily.

'Yes, my little ducks,' said Fidget. 'Of course, it would be a different matter if he'd come out in green spots. It seems Buster rescued him in the nick of a crab's claw.'

Fidget helped Ben to Buster's room and laid him down in the spare bed. Emily closed the curtains and went to find a flannel. She had read somewhere that cold flannels were good for headaches. Whether whirling eyes gave you headaches, or headaches gave you whirling eyes, Emily wasn't sure. When she came back, Ben was tucked up with

Doughnut lying at his feet. The little dachshund raised his head and opened one brown eye as if to say it was a hard life, being a guard dog.

'How long will Ben need to sleep?' asked Emily.

'A day should sort him out,' said Fidget. 'Then he'll be up and ready to go shrimping.'

Emily started to pin the photos she had taken on the wall.

'Should you be doing that?' said Buster. 'Joan won't be pleased.'

'This is an emergency,' said Emily. 'We're no closer to solving the crimes. Do you think other detectives worry about hotel walls when they're in the middle of a serious investigation?' She put up a sticky note with the name Herbie Snivelle written on it in red.

Buster and Fidget watched, mighty impressed, as Emily pinned up the e-fit of the broomstick, the photo of the purple bunny, a newspaper clipping about the car-showroom owner whose car had been shrunk, and a snap of Miss Pin's shop which she'd taken on the way back from the Scarycrow factory.

'Now what?' asked Buster.

Emily brought out some string and used it to make connections:

Herbie with the bunny rabbit . . .

. . . the bunny rabbit with the broomstick . . .

. . . the broomstick with Miss Pin's shop.

'It looks like cat's cradle,' said Fidget.

Emily had to agree that it did.

'It's supposed to help us think and make us see connections,' she said. 'It's what they do in detective programmes on TV. But I can't see a connection between the car shrinking and anything else. Perhaps there isn't one.'

'Wait a minnow,' said Fidget. 'I'm remembering something and it is to do with Herbie. Let me think.'

This was difficult for a cat whose mind was more given to fish-paste sandwiches and a good kip rather than trawling through his memories, which went back a very long way indeed. As far back, in fact, as the days of England's one and only Faerie Queene.

'I remember,' said Fidget at last. 'The Queen had been out saying hello to her people and she was about to return home when it was discovered that her carriage had been shrunk to the size of a doll's-house toy. The Faerie Queene was none too pleased, the road being mighty muddy. That was when that man whose name had something to do with water threw his cloak over a puddle so that the Queen's shoes wouldn't be ruined.'

Emily said, 'Are you talking about Sir Walter Raleigh?'

'Spot on the fishcake,' said Fidget. 'That's the chap.

An adventurer and a show off, if you ask me.'

'Wow,' said Emily. 'Did you really, really, really know Queen Elizabeth the first?'

'Yes, of course, but that has nothing to do with the case,' said Fidget. 'I only mention it because I remember the carriage was shrunk and who it was who did the shrinking. Connect that bit of string to Herbie.'

'Oh, very good,' said Buster. 'So Herbie already had a little thing about shrinking vehicles in the reign of Elizabeth the first?'

'That's right,' said Fidget.

Emily found a picture online of Sir Walter Raleigh, printed it off, pinned it to the wall and duly joined it with more pieces of string to the newspaper clipping of the car-showroom owner and to the sticky note that said Herbie Snivelle.

She put up stick drawings of the broomstick's two accomplices and joined them to the e-fit of the broomstick and the photo of Miss Pin's shop. By the time she had finished the wall had been transformed into a very colourful map. The three detectives were no closer to solving the crimes but it was painfully clear that Harpella had to be stopped from ever getting her broomstick back.

The magic lamp came into the room. Round its lid was a sleep mask with I Am a Star printed on it in silver.

'Has my agent called?' asked the magic lamp.

'No,' said Fidget.

'Oh, he will. The panto will be lost without me – lost, I tell you.' It gazed up at the pictures and bits of strings that Emily had so carefully pinned to the wall.

'That's very pretty,' said the lamp. 'I like the use of the modern with the historical. It captures the essence of–'

'Will you put a sock in it?' said Buster. 'This isn't art. It's a Think Board. We're looking for clues, joining things together, that kind of thing.'

'Still,' said the magic lamp, 'it's very pretty.'

Buster was about to say something about how unhelpful the magic lamp was and how little it realised the danger they were all in, when the bedroom door opened and there stood Ben.

The lamp let out a piercing scream. Ben's face, neck and hands were covered in bright green spots.

'Smelly jellyfish!' said Fidget. 'This is far worse than I first thought. It's harpeasles.'

'Is it catching?' asked Emily.

'Only if you're not a fairy, my little ducks.'

Chapter Fifteen

ravel felt his tummy to be full of wobbly jelly. He couldn't go back and tell the broomstick what had happened. It wouldn't for a minute believe him – and then what? Another brush up. Neither could he go to the police. Oh blimey, he thought, what shall I do? He walked forlornly up the High Street, looking for the gangster who had shrunk his van. It was useless. He dreaded facing Grim and the broomstick.

Gravel felt in need of a cup of tea. He was passing the Red Lion Hotel so he went inside. The tea room was very busy with a coach party having a day out from the city. There was only one table with any space and even that was occupied by a little girl wearing a knitted fish dress.

'If you don't mind sharing,' said the waitress, showing him to the table where the little girl was busy writing in a notebook.

'Do you mind if I sit here?' Gravel asked the girl.

Emily Vole glanced up.

'It's all right,' she said, and carried on scribbling.

Tea and cakes were brought to the table and Gravel, feeling a little calmer, asked Emily what she was writing.

'Notes on a case,' she said.

'Really,' said Gravel, smiling to himself. 'What are you – a budding detective?'

'Well, no, not budding. I am a detective,' said Emily, handing him a card.

It read:

Wings & Co
Fairy Detective Agency

'My name is Emily Vole.'

Aww, how sweet, thought Gravel, as he put four lumps of sugar in his tea and gave it a stir.

'Mine is Gravel,' he said. 'Do you mind my asking, are you good at solving crimes?'

'Yes,' said Emily. 'Why? Do you need a crime solving?'

That made Gravel smile again. He took a bite of a scone and watched as Emily went on with her notes.

Gravel thought it would be good to tell someone what was happening, and what harm could come of speaking the truth to this little girl? After all, the broomstick was the stuff of fairy tales.

'What would you say,' said Gravel, 'if I told you that my boss is a broomstick and a rather unpleasant one at that?'

Emily looked up at Gravel.

'I would say that was very interesting,' said Emily. 'What does this broomstick look like?'

'It's pink, has a bicycle seat in the middle, wears horn-rimmed glasses, has two arms with leather-gloved hands and gets through five packets of 2B pencils a day.'

Gravel expected Emily to burst out laughing. She didn't.

She said, 'Does the broomstick speak?'

'No. It's more given to walloping with its bristles when it's angry. Which it is most of the time. Oh – and it draws rather well.'

'Where is it at the moment, this broomstick?' said Emily.

'Blimey, you do ask very good questions,' said Gravel. If I tell her, he thought, and even if she tells someone else, who's going to believe her? Anyway, a trouble shared is a trouble spared or something like that.

So Gravel told Emily how they had found the broomstick half submerged in water, in a ditch, in a lay-by on a motorway.

'It's a pity we ever thought to rescue it.'

Emily made several notes and asked, 'Which motorway?'

'Is that important?' said Gravel.

'You need to be precise,' said Emily. 'Details are a vital part of a detective's job.'

Gravel chuckled. 'Of course. When I was a youngster I liked playing Cops and Robbers.'

'Which were you?'

'Robber,' said Gravel. 'You don't need to write that down.'

Emily had done so already.

'Go on,' she said. 'The motorway was . . . ?'

'The M94,' said Gravel.

'Then what?'

Gravel left out the bit about the robberies but he did tell her what had happened when he went to fill up his white transit van.

'I glanced out and saw my van shrink before my eyes and the man put it in a matchbox and just walked away. I ran after him but I couldn't find him anywhere.'

'What did he look like?' asked Emily.

'He was wearing a gangster suit with pinstripes, and a hat. And black-and-white shoes.'

Emily looked up.

'Have you by any chance seen a purple rabbit?'

'No,' said Gravel, laughing. Just as he'd thought, the kid saw it all as a fairy tale.

He was piling jam on another scone when he caught a glimpse of a middle-aged man and an elderly woman sitting a few tables away. There was something familiar about the man. Gravel knew he had seen him before – but where?

It was Sergeant Litton's day off and he was having tea with his mother. His mobile phone rang.

'No, Dumpty, said his mother firmly. 'Not at the table. I've told you, it's not polite.'

'But, Mumsy,' said Sergeant Litton, 'this might be important.'

'And I am not?' said Sergeant Litton's mother.

'This,' shouted the sergeant, 'is police work!'

'Dumpty, there is no need to raise your voice,' said his mother.

But the word POLICE had reached Gravel's ears and he stood up, and, leaving some money on the table, made a speedy exit.

'Wait,' called Emily, as he disappeared through the revolving doors. Emily grabbed her satchel and rushed out after him. Gravel had jumped in a taxi on the rank outside the hotel. Emily wavered a moment then leapt in the next one.

'Where to?' said the driver.

'Follow that taxi,' said Emily.

She'd always wanted to say that.

Herbie Snivelle had been hanging around outside the fire station all afternoon. He wanted a fire engine to add to his collection and it wasn't proving easy. Unlike car showrooms, the Fire Service didn't let people in to look at fire engines, which was a terrible pity. He was pondering what to do next when he spied across the street a shapely pair of chicken legs. He'd have known those chicken legs anywhere. Herbie pulled his hat down in the hope that Harpella hadn't seen him. This was a reunion he had spent the last four and a half centuries avoiding.

Of all the streets in all the towns in all the world, he thought, that crazy witch has to walk down this one. What was she doing in Podgy Bottom? Why now? He sidled off as fast as he could and ducked down the first alley he came to. Taking shelter in a doorway, he mopped his face with his hanky. After what felt like ages he had decided that the coast must be clear when the shadow of Harpella fell across him.

'Herbie Snivelle, you two-timing creep,' she said in a voice that was enough to turn his bones to stones. 'You owe me.'

'Good to see you, Chicken,' said Herbie. 'You're looking swell. Time hasn't changed you at all. If anything you're better looking now than when—'

Herbie didn't finish. Harpella had her red, steel fingernails around his neck.

'Don't . . . don't do this, Chicken,' said Herbie, as his feet left the ground. 'For old times' sake . . . howzabout we call a truce?'

'Only if you help me,' snarled Harpella.

'Anything, Chicken, just say the word.'

'The word is broomstick. And I want mine back.'

Chapter Sixteen

Emily hadn't an idea in seven where the taxis were going. They rushed through Podgy Bottom, street after street, none of which looked at all familiar, until Gravel's taxi stopped outside a car showroom.

NO FIBS FROM PHIBBS
The Best Deals On Four Wheels

Phibbs, thought Emily. She recognised the name from the newspaper cutting about the car-shrinking.

'Do you want to get out here?' said the taxi driver.

Emily wasn't sure what she should do and was regretting that she didn't have the mobile phone with her so she could call Fidget. She looked at the taxi's meter and counted her emergency pound coins. She had enough to ask the driver to wait, but Gravel was taking his time. Emily watched the meter tick-tick-ticking over. At last Gravel came out of the showroom followed by a man with a moustache. Whatever they were saying to one another, they seemed to be in great agreement. Gravel glanced in Emily's direction and she sank lower in her seat, hoping he hadn't seen her. He climbed into a white van on the forecourt and drove away.

'Follow that van,' said Emily.

They had soon left the outskirts of Podgy Bottom and the houses had fallen away. A road sign, which said 'Bosford 1 mile', meant nothing to her. It was here that the white van disappeared down a narrow turning. At about the same time, Emily's supply of pound coins ran out. Wishing she had enough to ask him to wait, she paid the taxi driver all the money she had and he drove off. Emily peered round the corner. She hoped to see the white van parked up and was very disappointed to find the cobbled lane empty. She was now so far from the Red Lion Hotel that she thought it was best to investigate what she could, even though there wasn't much to show for her desperate taxi ride. On one side of the lane was a high wall; the other side was lined with lock-up garages. Having walked down the lane and back Emily decided it was hopeless. She was wondering how she was going to get to Podgy Bottom when a voice called to her from above.

'What are you looking for?' the voice asked.

She looked up to see a freckled, ginger-haired boy of about ten staring down at her from a tree house.

'Did a white van come this way?' asked Emily.

'Might have done,' said the boy. 'Then again, might not have.'

'Oh, buddleia,' said Emily to herself as the boy disappeared into the tree's autumn leaves. 'Now what?'

The next thing she knew, she was nearly hit on the head by a rope ladder. On the bottom rung was a hastily written note. 'Come up,' it said.

Emily looked down the lane again and decided there was nothing to lose. She climbed the rope ladder and found herself in a very enviable den. The tree house had windows, a front door, two chairs and a table. On a shelf, alongside some books, was a pair of binoculars.

'Wow,' said Emily, truly impressed. 'This is some hideout.'

The boy put out his hand and said, 'My name is Alex.'

'And mine is Emily Vole.'

'Good to meet you,' said Alex. 'How can I help?'

'I'm doing some detective work,' said Emily.

Alex's face lit up.

'I want to be a detective when I'm grown up,' he said. 'What are you working on?'

'I've been following a white van.'

To Emily's great surprise, not only had Alex seen the van but he knew exactly which garage it had driven into. And, he added, it was a different van from the one that was usually kept there.

'I know that because I took down its registration number,' he said. 'And this one doesn't have Grim and Gravel on the side.'

Emily took her notebook from her satchel and wrote down all that Alex had to say, which was quite a lot.

He had taken photos with his birthday present, a Polaroid camera. To anyone except Emily they would have been of no interest whatsoever. They showed quite clearly Gravel and another man taking things out of the van and putting things into the garage.

'Can I keep these?' asked Emily. 'I promise to return them.'

'All right. But where do you live? Because I haven't seen you around.'

It was a tricky question and one Emily had discovered it was best to be vague about, so she said that at the moment she was staying at the Red Lion Hotel. Alex, who had never stayed anywhere apart from his gran's, was duly impressed.

'Are you staying there with your mum and dad?' he asked.

'No, with my
guardian,' said Emily.
'I couldn't use those
binoculars, could I?'

She imagined Alex would be a bit like Buster and say
'No' just for the sake of saying 'No'. Instead he handed
them to Emily. She peered through them and, to her
delight, the garage door opened a fraction. She waited,
hardly daring to breathe. It was then that the broomstick
swept out into the fading light. It stood upright and in
its leather-gloved hands it held a pencil. The broomstick
sharpened the lead down to a stub before swishing back
into the garage.

Emily handed the binoculars back to Alex.

'Thank you,' she said. She tucked Alex's Polaroids in her
notebook before returning everything to her satchel. 'I have
to go now.'

And then she remembered she was lost.

Chapter Seventeen

'I'm afraid we have a problem, Guv,' Poppy had said, closing the bonnet of the car.

Love temporarily overcame Detective Cardwell's sense of duty. He couldn't believe his luck. The problem meant that they had to spend a night in a nearby village while the garage tried to find a spare part that would fit the vintage engine. There was nothing for it but to book two rooms at the local pub. Never in a hundred years would James have thought a mechanical failure would give him the chance he had been longing for: to spend some time with the woman of his dreams.

That evening they sat in the pub near a roaring fire and ordered steak and kidney pie with chips and tomato sauce. The more they talked, the more they found how much they had in common. Poppy loved flying and had taken up gliding. She also had a fabulous memory and was able to talk about historical events as if she had actually been there. James hadn't met many women in the police service who liked history as much as Poppy did. She became rather vague when James asked about her family and only said that she had lost her father when she was very young and didn't remember him. James was equally vague when she asked him the same questions.

It was after their second ginger beer, as they were finishing the steak and kidney pies, that Poppy said, 'Guv . . .'

'Call me James, please.'

'James, there's something I've been meaning to tell you.'

'Yes?' said James, perched on the edge of his seat, wondering if his heart could be seen thumping through his shirt or, worse still, his wings flapping under his jacket.

'I know it's a bit out of line,' she said nervously.

'No – go on,' said James. 'I too have something to tell you.'

But neither of them told each other anything for at that very moment the pub door swung open and in

galumphed a retriever puppy. He headed straight for the remains of their steak and kidney pies, and in an explosion of golden ears and paws and tail, upset the table, sending chips, ginger beer and plates into the air. It took a while to sort out the mess and by then what they had planned to say to one another felt out of place, not to mention embarrassing.

In a motel room near Podgy Bottom, Herbie Snivelle wasn't feeling so good. There was a purple rabbit asleep on the bed. Even as a rabbit, Harpella was still the most terrifying dame he'd ever known. It took the shine off his shoes just hearing her speak. If a voice could make you feel small then his ex-wife made him feel matchbox-size. He'd decided that – for the time being at least – the best plan was to agree to all her demands.

Harpella had a plan and he was central to it. Herbie also had a plan and the purple rabbit who was once his wife was definitely not central to his. He had to find a way of getting rid of the witch once and for all. If only he could shrink her the way he shrank cars. But his powers were limited. It would be different if he had his wings back – at least he could fly away. For now he had to pretend he was still fond of the old chicken, even though the old chicken was a rabbit.

'I'll help you if you'll help me,' he'd said.

'I might,' said Harpella, as she'd hopped out of the robot the previous evening. 'Help you with what?'

Herbie had listed what he wanted: a stretch limo, a fire engine, and, most importantly, to be in charge of Wings & Co.

'First, let's run through the agenda for the Hallowe'en Ball,' said Harpella, munching yet another bunch of carrots.

'Why, Chicken? We've been through it a hundred times.'

'But you, Herbie, have a brain the size of a butterfly's and the memory of a gnat. So, tell me the plan.'

'We make a big entrance. While you distract the guests with your Scary Chicken Legs, I grab the broomstick – the one with the bicycle seat and the gloved hands.'

'Yes-yes-yes. Then what?' said Harpella, hopping up and down.

Herbie had forgotten the next part.

'Wait,' he said. 'How do you know this broomstick of yours will be there?'

'Because if there's one thing my broomstick loves more than anything, it's a good Hallowe'en party.'

'Couldn't you just find another broomstick, Chicken? There are a lot of them about this time of year.'

'That's the one thing I'd forgotten about you, Herbie Snivelle.'

'What's that?' said Herbie.

'Your limited imagination.'

There was something in the way Harpella looked at him when she spoke that made Herbie feel he was losing the plot.

'Hey, Chicken – remember how we met?' said Herbie, changing the subject.

Harpella's plan for the Hallowe'en Ball was giving him the heebie-jeebies.

'I do remember you shrank the Queen's carriage.'

'And I gave it to you as a token of my love,' said Herbie, stroking her bunny ears.

'Stop the whoozy, mushy flashbacks, just stick to the plan,' said Harpella. 'And DON'T touch me.'

'Sure, Chicken, sure,' said Herbie. 'I hear you – loud and clear.'

'Once I'm back to my old self,' said Harpella, 'we can re-

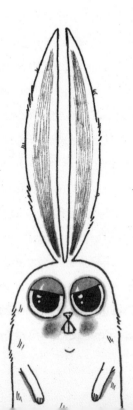

marry and start all over again. We can run Wings & Co together.'

Herbie gulped.

'Now, where were we?' said Harpella. 'Oh yes. We had just come to the best bit of my plan. When I have control of the broomstick, I will show them what a Hallowe'en can really be. Afterwards, I shall turn all the guests into . . .' She thought for a moment.

'Gerbils?' suggested Herbie.

'Yes, gerbils,' said Harpella. 'And this time they will stay that way. Then you and I will take off on the broomstick into a bat-filled sky.'

'I don't like bats.'

'Then you'll just have to close your eyes. But right now, you're going to buy two tickets for the ball and order a stretch limo to take us there.'

'Can I shrink it afterwards?' asked Herbie.

'You can turn it into a pumpkin for all I care.'

Herbie made for the door.

'Not so fast,' said Harpella. 'Where are you going?'

'To order the limo and—'

'NO. Pick up the phone like everyone else. It has taken me centuries to find you, Herbie Snivelle, and you are NOT SNEAKING AWAY FROM ME AGAIN. If you do, I will hunt you down and it will be fried fairy for you.'

'Chicken, babe – as if I would!'

Herbie's plan was simple. Grab the broomstick and make a run for it. If it had the power to undo a bunny spell, it might have the power to make Harpella disappear altogether. And that moth-eaten old cat too.

In fact, Herbie thought, as he watched his ex-wife sleep, the broomstick might make all his dreams come true.

Chapter Eighteen

The following morning, the garage phoned James Cardwell to say his car was ready and as good as new. Despite having an excellent breakfast together, James wished bitterly that it was last night and they were sitting across steak and kidney pies and Poppy was still calling him James not Guv. Most of all he wished that the blasted puppy had never set paw in the pub. It was sad to think that their short break together had ended without him knowing what it was Poppy wanted to tell him.

'Shall we go over the case, Guv?' said Poppy, who was driving.

'Ye-es,' said James dreamily, checking his phone. 'Oh, listen. Sergeant Litton has emailed about sightings of a scary robot in Podgy Bottom. Though the sergeant thinks it's nothing more than a publicity campaign for a Hallowe'en event. When is Hallowe'en?'

'Tomorrow, Guv,' said Poppy.

Sounds like more fairy mischief, thought James. As

usual, Sergeant Litton was barking up the wrong tree. He would have liked to discuss it with Poppy but, of course, he couldn't. Working with a non-fairy detective was going to be tricky.

'Drop me off at the Red Lion Hotel,' said James. 'And go on to the police station and get started on the car-shrinking case – review the evidence, interview witnesses.'

'Of course, Guv. Are you sure you won't need your car again?'

'No. Don't worry,' said James. 'I can always fly – I mean call a mini-cab. Or a helicopter. If it comes to it. Which it won't.'

He climbed out of the car and was certain he saw Poppy smile as she drove off.

James walked into the Atlantic Suite to find Emily covered in bright pink spots.

'Hello, Jimmy, my old cod,' said Fidget. 'We have a problem.'

'You can say that again,' said James.

'First Ben, then me,' said Emily. 'It's just not fair. I feel awful – all achy.'

The magic lamp rushed into the room holding a thermometer, a stethoscope bouncing on its golden tummy and a nurse's hat perched on its lid.

'My sweet mistress has come down with harpeasles, James. No non-fairy can be admitted to the suite; harpeasles is too contagious. Ben is in a far worse state. He's got green harpeasles. My mistress has the pink. I do think the pink is prettier.'

'You'd better tell me what's happened,' said James. 'Who's Ben?'

'First things first,' said Fidget. 'Emily needs to go to bed.' And he gently picked her up and carried her to her room, followed by a solemn procession of all seventeen keys.

'What exactly are they going to do?' asked Buster.

'Sit beside her bed of course, and weep,' said the magic lamp, trotting after the keys. 'What else do you think they're going to do?'

'It's back then,' said James to Buster.

'You know,' said Buster, 'it was really peaceful without it.'

The lamp closed the bedroom door firmly behind it.

'Yesterday, downstairs in the tea room,' said Buster, 'Emily met a man called Gravel who said his boss was a broomstick. She followed him in a taxi and spotted the broomstick outside a lock-up garage near Bosford. Some boy got his mother to drive her back here. Oh, and Gravel bought a van from Phibbs, whose Thunderbird was shrunk. Take a look at our Think Board. It shows all the connections.'

James went to the Think Board and prodded the sticky note on which Emily had written the name 'Herbie Snivelle'.

'How does he fit in?' he asked.

Not long after lunch, James's mobile rang. It was Poppy. She had driven round all the hotels and B&Bs in the neighbourhood and discovered the whereabouts of a man who matched the description of the car-shrinker.

'Good,' said Detective Cardwell, somewhat surprised at her fast work. 'Is his name Herbie Snivelle, by any chance?'

'Yes,' said Poppy. 'How did you know?'

'Oh, I'll tell you later. Where is he?'

'At the Flotsam Creek Motel. It's just outside Podgy Bottom. Shall we go and take a look, Guv? I could pick you up in your car.'

'No,' said James, more firmly than he intended. 'No, that's not a good idea.'

'But, Guv, this is our main suspect, we need to move fast.'

'I think,' said James, 'you should . . . er . . . go and have a cup of tea. I'll apply for a search warrant.'

'Tea? But Guv . . .'

'I'll see you tomorrow, Detective Perkins.'

And before Poppy could say another word James ended the call.

It took Detective Cardwell quite a while to get a search warrant for the Flotsam Creek Motel. But everything took longer in Podgy Bottom. It was growing dark by the time Sergeant Litton picked him up.

'I have all the right papers,' he said.

James was not in the best of moods. 'The suspect could be halfway to Scotland by now,' he said.

'I doubt that,' said Sergeant Litton. 'There are no trains leaving Podgy Bottom today. Mr Robertson's sheep escaped this morning and are still wandering up and down the line.'

'That, at least, is good news,' said Detective Cardwell. 'But Mr Robinson's sheep haven't stopped cars and buses and every other means of transport from running, I take it?'

Sergeant Litton wasn't listening. His tummy was rumbling. As usual he was feeling a bit peckish.

'Do you think we could stop at the Hungry Horse? It does a very good beef burger. Mother says it's horse meat, though I doubt that.'

'No,' said Detective Cardwell. 'We're not stopping for beef, horse or gerbil burger.'

The Flotsam Creek Motel was a seedy-looking place that had seen better days. There was no one on the reception desk but above it was a sign that read 'Smile – You Are On Camera'. Detective Cardwell rang the bell several times before finally a woman appeared.

James said, 'I'm Detective Cardwell and I have . . .' but he didn't finish what he was saying because the woman rushed up to Sergeant Litton and lifted him off his feet.

'If it isn't little Dumpty come to say hello to his Auntie Enid!' she said. 'Has his Mumsie forgiven me then?'

'Dumpty?' said James.

'Auntie Enid, please. I'm here on police business,' said Sergeant Litton.

'I could have done with you here earlier, I can tell you,' said the motel receptionist.

'Why?' asked James.

'Because one of my guests did a runner, that's why. Left without paying the ruddy bill.'

'What was his name?' asked James, fairly sure of the answer.

Enid looked in the register which, like the motel, was a mess. 'Can't read my own writing,' she said, screwing up her face. 'Hippo Snot. Could that be it?'

'Herbie Snivelle?' said Detective Cardwell helpfully.

'Oh yes, that's it,' said Enid. 'Yes, Hippo, Herbie, they all sound the same to me. That nice policewoman was asking about him. He wore a gangster suit and had a pet rabbit – purple and as big as a rottweiler. I've never seen a rabbit that large. It had pink ears.'

'Hippo Snot had pink ears?' said Sergeant Litton.

'No, Dumpty dear, do try to keep up. The rabbit had pink ears.'

The knowledge that Herbie and Harpella were back together sent a shiver of dread through James. It was bad enough that those two had met up again, but the thought of what might happen to Wings & Co if they found the broomstick was truly terrifying. That, he knew, must not happen.

'You all right?' said Enid. 'You've gone as pale as a snowstorm.'

'Could we see the room?' asked Detective Cardwell. 'We have a warrant.'

'Be my guest,' said Enid. 'I haven't had a chance to clean up yet.' She fetched the keys and showed them where Herbie Snivelle had been staying. 'Dumpty,' she whispered to her nephew, 'I've just made meringues with whipped cream.'

'Detective Cardwell, I think I should investigate the kitchen,' said the sergeant.

James couldn't care less what Sergeant Litton investigated. He was about as useful as an umbrella with a hundred holes in it.

'Go ahead,' he said.

James snapped on a pair of latex gloves and thoroughly searched the motel room. There were plenty of purple rabbit hairs but nothing else of interest. He was about to leave when he spotted something white gleaming in the folds of the pink nylon valance. It was a tiny van. On its sides it said,

Grim & Gravel

No Job Too Small or Too Large

Chapter Nineteen

That night, when most sensible people were tucked up in bed, the broomstick was to be found at the lock-up garage on its tenth packet of 2B pencils. It had been going through the final checklist of all that was needed for the bank robbery. Grim and Gravel were dressed in black, both clutching their balaclavas, Grim twiddling his pom-pom. Both looked nervous. The broomstick showed them the comic strip again and made sure they understood exactly what they had to do and when.

A few miles away in Podgy Bottom, Maureen Pin decided Hellman needed to stretch his legs. Maureen didn't sleep much, not since her husband had died, and anyway it was a good excuse for her to check on her daughter's shop. She had been very worried about security since the robbery.

She quietly closed the front door and walked down the avenue in the rain to Podgy Bottom High Street. She arrived at the shop just as the white van carrying Grim, Gravel and the broomstick pulled up on the opposite side of the road. The broomstick wound down the window and nudged Gravel in the ribs, pointing to the lady with the dog.

'I don't know who that is,' said Gravel.

'Neither do I,' said Grim.

The broomstick watched the lady let herself into the shop and turn on a light.

'Perhaps, Boss,' said Grim, 'we should do this another night.'

The broomstick grabbed hold of him, opened the van door and pushed him out into the street. For a non-talking broomstick, the message was loud and clear: there would be no backing down now. Gravel watched as Grim was broomhandled to the shop door.

Maureen Pin, seeing all was well, had decided to make herself a cup of tea, when her dog started yapping. She went back into the shop and saw a broomstick in the doorway.

'Trick-or-treating isn't until tomorrow, so scarper before I call the police,' she said.

Grim was hiding in the changing room and at that

moment, he sneezed. Maureen Pin grabbed the phone
but the broomstick was coming towards her, its arms
outstretched. The little dog charged
and bit it on the handle. Pink
sparks flew from the bristles and
zoomed towards Mrs Pin. Grim
saw the lady and the dog
frizzling round the edges,
then all was silent.

Gravel, still sitting in the van, was alarmed to see pink sparks light up the shop window. There were no pink sparks in the broomstick's careful comic-strip plan. He began to feel more and more nervous as the minutes ticked by. Finally, Grim came out and ran across the road.

'Where's the broomstick?' said Gravel.

'I left it in the basement,' said Grim, getting into the van. 'We need to get away – and fast.'

'Why?' asked Gravel.

'That broomstick has terrible powers.' Grim was shaking. 'He can turn us into pumpkins.'

'Don't be daft,' said Gravel.

'I'm not joking. Look,' said Grim, holding out his hands. 'I'm a trembling wreck.'

At that moment the bank's alarm went off and both of them jumped, hitting their heads on the roof of the van.

Gravel started the van.

'Put your foot on the accelerator and let's go,' said Grim. 'NOW.'

But Gravel found that though the wheels were going round, the van wasn't moving. Turning his head he came face to face with the furious broomstick, sparks flying, its leather-gloved hand on the door handle, holding back the van.

'Oh – hello, boss,' said Gravel. 'Didn't see you there.'

He kept the engine running while Grim shakily climbed out and opened the rear doors. Quickly, he and the broomstick loaded the van with money and then, the bank's alarm still wailing, the three robbers drove away.

Sergeant Litton didn't like being woken in the middle of the night. It upset Mumsy and she needed her beauty sleep. Slowly he dressed, brushed his teeth and tucked up his teddy in bed before driving into town to see what was going on at Podgy Bottom's bank.

He arrived there ten minutes after Gravel had driven away. There was no sign of a break-in. It was just another faulty alarm. These modern alarms were always going off without cause. All he had to do was wait for the bank manager and see if this was anything serious.

He sat in his police car and stared at the clothes shop opposite. In the window was a display made out of pumpkins. Clever idea, that, thought Sergeant Litton. They look exactly like Miss Pin's mother and that yapping dog of hers.

The bank manager arrived in his dressing gown and was very flustered as he unlocked the bank vaults.

'Oh no,' he said. 'We've been robbed. Do something.'

Sergeant Litton could hardly believe it. After all, nothing much ever happened in Podgy Bottom. The idea that he had to do something sent him into a spin.

'Perhaps we should call the police,' he said.

It wasn't until the following morning that Karen Pin discovered that her mother and the dog were missing. She couldn't imagine where they might have gone. It looked as if her mother's bed hadn't been slept in. Karen put on her coat and was about to go out to look for her when there was a loud knock on her front door.

'Mum, where have you been?' said Karen, as she opened the door.

But it wasn't her mother, it was Sergeant Litton.

'You had better come with me,' he said. 'There has been an incident at your shop.'

Chapter Twenty

After a frustrating day in Podgy Bottom, Poppy had decided she should be honest with James. How could they work together when neither of them was being truthful to the other? It was time she told him about a private investigation she'd been working on, one that had a lot to do with Wings & Co.

She would also have liked to have told him, when she'd had the chance, that her heart beat much faster when he was around. Except she hadn't and now it was all too late. Since they'd arrived in Podgy Bottom, James had been doing his best to avoid her. He hadn't even informed her he'd learned the name of the suspect in the Matchbox Mysteries. If they weren't a team, they would never solve the case. More important still, what would happen if Doctor Dreadalpan and Harpella found each other? She feared there would be a terrible showdown. Harpella wanted to be the witch she had been before she was turned into a rabbit, and Doctor

Dreadalpan wanted to be the alchemist he was before Harpella had changed him into a broomstick.

She had called James to ask if they could have breakfast to review the case. There was something she urgently needed to speak to him about. James had sounded flustered and said it would have to be early as he was dealing with a personal matter.

'Oh,' said Poppy. And a worrying thought crossed her mind. Maybe there was a lady in James's life and she had just been fooling herself into thinking there was a spark between them.

'I am a chump,' she said to herself. 'A right chump. We are just colleagues, nothing more.'

She set off in James's car from the B&B where she had spent the night. As she waited at the traffic lights she read a sign in a sweet shop window. It said, The best tricks, the best treats in town.

Poppy hated Hallowe'en. It was all wrong, children dressed up as ghoulies and ghosties, begging for sweets. Meanwhile their doting parents looked on as if it was fine and dandy for their little darlings to go knocking on doors, threatening neighbours with goodness knows what if there wasn't a treat in store.

She arrived in Podgy Bottom, parked the car and went into the hotel. The place was in an uproar of Hallowe'en

Ball preparations.

'Can I help you?' said Joan the receptionist.

'Yes,' said Poppy. 'I'm meeting Detective Cardwell. Is he here?'

Joan, distracted by all the comings and goings, said, 'Give me a moment and I'll phone the Atlantic Suite.'

And with that she disappeared into the office.

Poppy wasn't in a waiting mood. She'd find James herself. She took the lift to the second floor and as she walked along the corridor she noticed a maid cleaning the rooms. She was wearing headphones and dancing to some unheard pop song.

She knocked on the door of the Atlantic Suite. It was opened by a boy of about eleven.

'Yes?' he said. 'What do you want?'

'Is Detective Cardwell here?'

'No,' said the boy. 'He said he had a breakfast meeting and had to leave. Who are you?'

'I'm Poppy Perkins, Detective Cardwell's assistant. May I come in and wait?'

To her surprise the boy said abruptly, 'No,' then added, 'we have two seriously contagious people here and they are in isolation.'

Before Poppy could say another word the boy had closed the door. An idea came to her. While the maid went

to fetch more towels from the laundry cupboard, Poppy
seized her chance. She sneaked into one of the empty
rooms and let herself out onto the balcony. The Red Lion
Hotel was a Georgian building with a wrought-iron
balcony stretched across its front. It was just a matter
of working out which of the rooms belonged to the
Atlantic Suite.

She came to one in which a little girl sat propped
up in bed, reading a book. She was covered in bright pink
spots.

Poppy tried not to be seen but the girl waved at her.
Feeling somewhat silly, she waved back.

The little girl got out of bed and, as cool as a
cucumber, opened the balcony door.

'What are you doing there?' she asked.

'I'm Poppy Perkins, Detective Cardwell's assistant and
I . . .' She had to think for a minute. Oh, what was the
point? 'Are you Detective Cardwell's daughter?'

'No,' said Emily, laughing. 'He's a friend of ours.'

Poppy was rather surprised to find that her heart felt
lighter.

Emily explained that she was very contagious and it
wasn't a good idea for Poppy to come in.

'Well, if I stay out here, I'll get soaked.' Which was true;
it had started to rain quite hard. Once inside, she said, 'Are

you anything to do with the fairy detective agency?'

'Yes,' said Emily, putting on her dressing gown and slippers. 'I'm Emily Vole.'

How stupid, thought Poppy. What sort of detective am I? I should have worked that out.

'Of course, you're the Keeper of the Keys,' said Poppy. 'I need to speak to you. It's very important.'

At that moment Buster put his head round Emily's door.

'I ordered room service – tea, biscuits and cakes. You'd better come quickly before I eat them all up. Oh,' he said, seeing Poppy. 'What are you doing here? You can't just come barging in. Emily is contagious and is in isolation.'

'It's harpeasles, isn't it?' said Poppy.

Emily and Buster looked at Poppy with interest.

'How do you know that?' said Buster.

'Don't worry, I'm immune. You must be Buster Ignatius Spicer,' she said, holding out her hand.

'Did James tell you about the harpeasles?' said Buster.

'Not exactly,' said Poppy. She followed Buster and Emily into the sitting room and was impressed to see the Think Board on the wall. 'Who did this?' she asked. 'It's very good.'

'I did,' said Emily. 'It's to help us work out what's going on.'

'And has it?' asked Poppy.

'A bit,' said Emily.

Poppy studied the pictures and then, from her shoulder-bag, took out a photograph.

'Would it be all right if I put this up? It might help.'

'What is it?' asked Emily.

'It's a photo of the villain I've been after for years,' said Poppy. 'It used to work for the witch Harpella. But in its own right it's just as powerful, if not more powerful than the witch herself.'

'It's the broomstick,' said Buster.

Emily went nearer and read the words under the photo.

'Dr Dreadalpan,' she said. 'But it's Harpella's broomstick.'

'Dr Dreadalpan was an alchemist,' said Poppy.

'What's that?' said Emily.

'Like a magician crossed with a chemist,' said Poppy. 'Harpella changed him into a broomstick and he has always wanted revenge. And of course, to be changed back into an alchemist. Harpella, on the other hand, needs Dr Dreadalpan to break the spell that made her a bunny rabbit.'

'Does James know all this?' asked Buster.

'No, not yet. I haven't found the right moment to tell him.'

'James thinks you're like Emily,' said Buster.

'Yes,' said Poppy. 'I'm just like Emily.'

'And you are . . . ?' said Buster.

'A detective. Like Emily. And we must catch Doctor Dreadalpan before Harpella does.'

Chapter Twenty-One

Sergeant Litton was baffled by the robbery at Podgy Bottom's bank, and had asked Detective Cardwell to take a look at the crime scene. James was examining a thin hole in the wall of the vaults. It was one brick wide and 140 centimetres high. Only a stick-man could have got through it. No explosives had been used to blow the safe, but the lock looked like molten toffee. James's wings were fluttering under his coat. More signs of fairy meddling.

'An inside job,' said Sergeant Litton sleepily. 'I mean, no one could've done it except the bank manager. Shall I arrest him?'

'Definitely not,' said Detective Cardwell.

'I've asked Karen Pin to talk to you. She's in her shop having a cup of tea,' said Sergeant Litton. 'She can't work out who would make such a realistic sculpture of her mother and her mother's dog out of pumpkins. Any suggestions?'

'The bank manager?' said James through gritted teeth. He had enough on his hands: Herbie Snivelle and the car-shrinking, the shop boarded up, two humans with harpeasles . . . and then there was Poppy.

'I should definitely arrest him,' said Sergeant Litton.

'No,' said James.

He sighed. He wished Poppy were there. She'd be good at handling Sergeant Litton.

No more messing around. When he saw her he would tell her the truth. He needed her.

Buster left Poppy and Emily together to go through all the clues on the Think Board. Buster had also been thinking, or rather remembering, a long-forgotten fact about Herbie Snivelle.

Buster put Doughnut on his lead and announced he was taking the dog for a walk. He looked in on Ben, who was still fast asleep, then the magic lamp. It was on the phone to its agent, the keys sitting safely at its side.

'Keep an eye on things while I'm out,' said Buster.

The magic lamp put its hand over the phone. 'Oh, I will. As usual. Just me, caring for everyone while you go out.'

Buster sighed and closed the door.

The lobby of the Red Lion Hotel was completely altered. Joan had bought tins of cobweb spray and a job lot of bats. All morning she had been up and down ladders. Not a column or post had been missed by her eager spray can. Bats dangled everywhere. Buster hardly recognised the place. It looked as if it belonged in a rather bad horror film.

'What do you think?' asked Joan, looking upon the gloomy scene she'd created.

Buster, who had fought his way through the cobwebs to the reception desk, thought perhaps it was best to say nothing.

'We were to have had a party organiser do this,' said Joan. 'But he was taken poorly yesterday, so I said I'd give it a bash. I always fancied myself as an interior designer. I have a way with Christmas trees.'

'I can see you might,' said Buster.

Through the mist of cobwebs, he could just make out the TV in the lounge. It was showing a local news item about the robbery at Podgy Bottom's bank. James was with Sergeant Litton, who was giving a press briefing.

So that's where he is, thought Buster.

'Well, come on, what do you think?' asked Joan again, as she came out from behind her desk. She was wearing a jumper with a light-up skeleton on it.

'I think you might have overdone the bats,' said Buster.

'Mmm. You may be right,' said Joan.

Buster stood outside the hotel and wondered about saving time by flying to the bank to see James. But Joan waved at him as she removed some bats from the hotel door and he thought better of it.

Miss Pin's shop was cordoned off with police tape and brown paper had been stuck to the inside of the shop window, hiding the pumpkin sculptures from view. Doughnut spotted James, rushed under the police tape and leapt into the detective's arms.

'That dog could be arrested for accosting a police officer,' said Sergeant Litton. 'Might I suggest, my lad, that you keep that hound under control?'

'Buster,' said James, taking no notice of Sergeant Litton. 'Am I glad to see you.'

'I take it,' interrupted Sergeant Litton, 'that you know this young man – and the dog?'

'Yes,' said James. 'Buster is my cousin. The dog is called Doughnut.' He pulled Buster away from the sergeant towards the shop. 'You are just the person I need. Come and see this.'

Sergeant Litton followed them.

'Detective Cardwell, we can't have children or dogs involved in police inquiries. What next? Gerbils?'

Inside the shop, Karen Pin was waiting.

James introduced himself.

'Nothing was stolen,' said Karen. 'I've checked my stock. But my window display is quite different. The pumpkins weren't there before. Anyway, I'm much more worried about Mum. Is there any news?'

Buster was taking a closer look at the pumpkin sculptures.

'Is this what I think it is?' whispered Buster to James.

'I am afraid so. It looks like her mum and the dog have been pumpkinated,' said Detective Cardwell quietly. 'Let me show you something else.'

In the shop's basement, he pointed to a tall, narrow hole in the wall between the racks of clothes.

'It would take a very thin stick-man to get through there,' said James.

'I suspect,' said Buster, 'that this is the work of Doctor Dreadalpan, better known to you and me as Harpella's broomstick.'

'How on earth do you know that?' asked James.

'Poppy,' said Buster.

'As in Detective Poppy Perkins, my assistant?'

'Are there fields of poppies in your life, James? Or just the Poppy you were supposed to meet for breakfast?'

'Oh, buddleia,' said James. 'Did she phone you? And how does she know about Doctor Dreadalpan?

'I don't know.' Buster smiled innocently at James. 'She turned up at the Atlantic Suite this morning looking for you. As a matter of fact, that's where she is now,' he said. 'With Emily.'

It hit James like a wet kipper on a Monday.

'Oh, no – she can't be!'

'But she is,' said Buster, enjoying seeing James in a tiz. One good thing about being eleven for a hundred years, he thought, was not growing up such a fool as to fall in love and go all soapy.

'She just sort of let herself in,' said Buster. 'She's a very determined woman.'

'Where was Fidget?' said James. 'Why didn't he stop her?'

'Because he went off this morning to see Alfred Twizzell.'

'I have to go straight back to the Red Lion Hotel,' said James. 'Poppy is in great danger of catching harpeasles.'

'Actually,' said Buster, 'I don't think she is.'

Chapter Twenty-Two

The morning after the bank robbery, while Grim and Gravel unloaded the van, the broomstick surfed the internet. It was searching for local shops that sold broomsticks and bicycle seats.

'You don't think the boss has lost the plot?' said Grim.

'Boss?' hissed Gravel. 'What have we come to, calling a broomstick "Boss"? We're supposed to be self-employed petty crooks and here we are, working full-time robbing banks for a master criminal.'

They looked up as the broomstick beckoned them over. Nervously they went to look at the screen.

'"Doctor Dreadalpan,"' read Gravel, '"was an alchemist in the court of Queen Elizabeth the first."'

'Alchemist? What's that when it's at home?' asked Grim.

Gravel read on.

'It says here that alchemists searched for the secret of turning ordinary household metal into gold and silver.'

'Blimey, that would be useful,' said Grim. 'You'd get the loot without the bank-robbing bit. What else does it say?'

'They also searched for the elixir of everlasting life,' said Gravel.

'The what?' said Grim.

'It's like an energy drink,' said Gravel, 'that makes you live for ever.'

'What's the boss got to do with this Doctor Dreadalpan?' said Grim.

The broomstick pointed to the name on the screen and then to itself.

'You?' said Gravel. 'You're Doctor Dreadalpan?'

The broomstick bowed.

'And you were born all those hundreds of years ago?'

Doctor Dreadalpan bowed again.

Grim gulped and said, 'I don't ever want to drink that elixir drink if it turns me into a blooming broomstick.'

He wished he hadn't said that as the broomstick pulled his ears quite hard.

Gravel thought to himself, I've had enough of this. I want to turn over a new leaf, be the good guy for a change.

With its index finger Doctor Dreadalpan beckoned him closer.

'What is it, Boss – I mean, Doctor?' said Gravel, who had a nasty feeling that the broomstick knew what he'd been thinking. To prove the point, it waggled its finger in front of him. The meaning of the gesture was quite plain: No, no, no.

Gravel felt in his pocket.

'Boss, Boss, you've got it all wrong,' he said. Triumphantly, he pulled out the leaflet about the Hallowe'en Ball. 'I was just thinking that it's Hallowe'en tonight and there's this ball at the Red—'

The broomstick grabbed the leaflet and read it. The two crooks had never seen it so excited. It started jumping up and down on the spot. Then it took out one of its pencils and began to draw. The two crooks looked on.

'Doctor Boss doesn't half do lovely pictures,' said Grim, a little carried away by the broomstick's sketches, although he scratched his head and had to think for a bit about what it all meant. The broomstick had drawn two white vans, one with a question mark beside it; a hardware shop and a bicycle shop; and two skeletons.

Gravel understood all too well what the drawings meant.

'The first van was shrunk, Boss,' he said.

The broomstick rotated its gloved hand, which meant, 'Go on.'

'By a man in a gangster suit. He wore dark glasses and a fedora hat and had a water pistol.' The broomstick started to draw again. 'That's him all right,' said Gravel, impressed. 'That's the man who shrunk my van.'

The broomstick rubbed its hands together and, for a non-smiling bicycle seat, the broomstick appeared to positively beam. It grabbed hold of Grim and Gravel and opened the van door.

'What about the dosh?' said Grim, looking sadly at the bags of money they had just unloaded.

The broomstick pointed to its drawing. Gravel started the engine and drove the van out of the lock-up and back into town. He turned on the radio. The local radio station was full of the news of the bank robbery. The broomstick turned up the volume when he heard the newsreader mention Detective James Cardwell. As they pulled up outside the hardware shop, it took out another 2B pencil and sharpened it threateningly.

Grim was sent in to buy thirty broomsticks and he got some funny looks as he loaded them into the van. Next he was sent to buy thirty bicycle seats and got even more funny looks. On the way out of town they stopped again, this time at a shop selling fancy-dress costumes. Grim was sent in to buy two skeleton outfits, one for him and the other for Gravel.

They pulled up outside the lock-up garage and unloaded the goods. None of them noticed the boy with binoculars watching them from his tree house.

Once the broomsticks and bicycle seats were stacked inside the garage and the door was shut, the broomstick drew what they were to do next.

Grim and Gravel spent the rest of the day screwing thirty bicycle seats to thirty broom handles.

Grim propped the last one against the inside of the garage door with all the others.

'They look daft,' he said, then seeing the boss bristle, added, 'I mean – they don't have your personality.'

The broomstick brushed Grim aside and stood in front of the thirty broomsticks as if he was about to conduct an orchestra. Grim and Gravel backed away as sparks began to fly from the broomstick's bristles.

It was then that the two crooks stopped being scared of the boss and became completely terrified. Before their eyes, each of the broomsticks came to life until there was an army of them, thirty strong.

'Oh, heck,' said Grim. 'What next?'

Chapter Twenty-Three

Later that morning, Emily received a call from Alex, who was keeping watch on the lock-up garage from his tree house. He had seen the white van leave earlier with two men and the broomstick. They had returned with a van full of broomsticks and bicycle seats.

'Thanks, Alex. Keep reporting back,' said Emily. 'And whatever you do, don't go near the garage.'

'All right. Will you be coming to the tree house?' Alex asked.

Emily caught a glimpse of herself in the mirror. Her pink spots looked brighter than ever, if that was possible.

'No,' she said sadly.

Poppy was waving at her.

'Wait a mo,' said Emily to Alex. 'What is it?' she asked Poppy.

'Tell him I'll be there as soon as I can.'

'Alex, I'm sending Detective Poppy Perkins. She's from Scotland Yard.'

'Wow. That's pretty cool. How will I know her?'

Emily looked at Poppy and said, 'You won't mistake her, that's for sure.'

Poppy put her bag over her shoulder and gave Emily a kiss.

'I think we've done well this morning,' she said.

'It's just a bundle of a nuisance that I can't come with you,' said Emily.

Poppy was about to leave when the magic lamp wandered in.

'I'm so-o-o-o bored,' it said. 'I haven't been out for days. DAYS, I tell you.'

'I'll take you with me if you want,' said Poppy.

'Oh, sweet lady,' said the magic lamp, going all shy. 'Why, to accompany you would be delightful. And I am a bright light in a tight corner.'

Emily wasn't sure that the magic lamp going with Poppy was a good idea.

'Shouldn't you stay by the phone, in case your agent calls?' she said.

'No, no. He called and I told him I have relinquished the stage.'

'What does "relinquished" mean?' asked Emily.

'It means that, with regret, I have retired from the theatre. I have given up all hope of being an actor. Sadly, I won't be making a comeback, not now, not ever.'

'I could do with the company,' said Poppy, trying not to laugh. 'Can you manage without the magic lamp for an hour or so?'

'Of course,' said Emily.

She watched from the window as Poppy put the magic lamp in the passenger seat of the Austin Healey and strapped the seat belt round it before sliding into the driver's seat.

'Buddleia,' said Emily to herself. 'I would love to go with them.'

Half an hour later, Buster and James and Doughnut returned to the Red Lion Hotel. To Buster's eyes, the lobby now looked even worse than it did before. There were pumpkins everywhere, carved into the shape of crazy bunny rabbits and looking more frightening than a spider in the bath.

'It's Mr Flower's little hobby,' said Joan. 'For some strange reason, he loves carving rabbits.'

'I have a bad feeling,' said James, inspecting a rabbit pumpkin, 'that his Hallowe'en Ball might attract the wrong sort of guest. Doctor Dreadalpan, for instance.'

'Or a purple bunny after her broomstick. Wow. This is

157

going to be a party to remember,' said Buster.

They went in the lift up to the Atlantic Suite.

'Where's Poppy?' said James to Emily, looking wildly around the room as if she might be hiding behind the curtains.

'She's gone to the lock-up garage where I saw the broomstick, AKA Doctor Dreadalpan,' said Emily, busy on the laptop.

'Buddleia and bindweed!' said James. 'She's in real danger. Why didn't you stop her, Emily? Why didn't the magic lamp stop her?'

'Because the magic lamp went with her.'

'Emily, you know perfectly well that at any moment Poppy will come down with harpeasles.'

'She won't,' said Emily.

James was beginning to lose his temper.

'Of course she will. You caught it from Ben and she'll catch it from you.'

Emily had never seen James so cross.

'Really, James, she won't,' she said.

'She can't,' said Buster. 'For a Scotland Yard detective you're not being very quick. You should've worked it out by now. I have.'

'Worked out what?' said James.

'That she's a fairy,' said Buster and Emily together.

James sat down with a thump.

'She told me she was born in the 1770s,' said Emily, 'in the reign of King George the third.'

James was quiet for a moment, then he said. '1776 . . .'

'The American Declaration of Independence,' said Emily. She loved history.

'No,' said James. 'I mean, yes, but . . . 1776 was the year Herbie Snivelle went to America.'

'I hate to mention it, but Miss String told me that Herbie left behind a baby daughter,' said Buster.

'Oh dear,' said Emily. 'Herbie told Fidget he'd left two sets of wings at Wings & Co – his and his baby's. Do you think that Poppy could possibly be . . .'

Before anyone said another word, Emily's mobile phone rang.

'Hi, Emily,' said Poppy. 'Put me on video.' And there was Poppy, smiling at them with not one spot on her face. 'I'm at the lock-up garage and I think I've located Doctor Dreadalpan.'

James grabbed the phone.

'Poppy, listen to me. You are to leave the area immediately. It's not safe and . . . and . . . we need to talk. Where's the magic lamp?'

Poppy moved the phone. James could see the magic

lamp peering through a crack in a garage door.

'Get the lamp and leave right now, that's an order,' shouted James into the phone.

Poppy turned the screen back to herself.

'Sorry, Guv,' she said. 'I can't hear you – you're breaking up.'

Behind her, Emily, Buster and James could see what Poppy couldn't see: the garage door was opening. The broomstick came gliding out.

'Poppy, behind you!' said James.

'What? Hello . . . oh, this phone . . . hello, hello, can you hear me?'

'Behind you!' shouted Emily and Buster.

'Poppy, LEAVE NOW!' said James.

Too late. The broomstick's gloved hand was over Poppy's mouth. There was a struggle and the phone fell to the ground. Briefly, the fairy detectives saw a wobbly shot of Poppy's shoes and the broomstick's handle.

They heard the magic lamp wail, 'Poppy, Poppy, NOOOO!'

And the screen went blank.

Chapter Twenty-Four

idget had spent the day visiting his old friend, Alfred
Twizzell. They hadn't seen each other for ages
and there had been much to catch up on. Over a lunch
of smoked mackerel, they talked of the old days, when
Alfred had worn a ruff and been an important figure in
Elizabethan England.

Afterwards, they dozed by the fire in Alfred's library
until Fidget woke with a start and realised that there was
very little time before he caught his train and he had
forgotten to ask all the questions he had come to ask.

'I'm here on three very important matters,' said Fidget.

'Yes?' said Alfred. 'What can I help you with?'

'Number one, broomsticks, number two, potions, and
number three, the shop,' said Fidget. 'So, first I need to
know about Harpella's broomstick.'

Alfred climbed up his library steps and took down a
book called Who's Who of Broomsticks. He flicked through
the pages until he found what he was looking for.

'"The Witch Harpella",' he read out. 'Oh dear, oh dear.'

'I don't like the tuna of that,' said Fidget.

'Brace yourself,' said Alfred. He continued reading. '"It is believed that the Witch Harpella's broomstick cannot be classed as a true broomstick."'

'What does that mean?' said Fidget. 'It sounds mighty fishy to me.'

'It says here that Harpella is rumoured to have changed a certain Doctor Dreadalpan into a broomstick.'

'You don't mean the alchemist and wizard?' said Fidget.

'Yes, I do. Let me read it again and see if there's anything I've missed out.' Alfred Twizzell picked up a magnifying glass and peered at the letters. 'This fairy's handwriting is very small. But that's what it says. Any help?'

'Yes,' said Fidget.

'Now, where is that book on wizards?' Alfred Twizzell's bookshelves reached as high as his ceiling. Several books were flying around the room and two huge volumes had taken to playing hide and seek rather noisily along the top shelves. 'I was left those by dear Ottoline String,' said Alfred. 'This happens all the time. They just fly off and find another shelf to hide on. How Ottoline ever kept them in order, I will never know.'

'We have the same problem in the library at Wings &
Co,' said Fidget. 'But Emily's very good with them.'

With great difficulty, Alfred managed to catch Volume
II of Wizards Through the Ages.

'As I thought. Doctor Dreadalpan went missing after a
meeting with Harpella in 1613. The wizard was never seen
again. That night, his servants left his house claiming they
had been chased away by a broomstick and when—'

Fidget interrupted him. 'I have to go, Alfred, or I'm
going to miss my train. But broomsticks and wizards
are not the only reason I'm here. You see, I should have
mentioned this first, but it is a bit embarrassing. Emily has
caught harpeasles and I need to know if there's a remedy.'

'How did she catch it?' asked Alfred, alarmed. 'That
should never have been allowed to happen.'

'I know, my old cod, I feel very bad about it,' said
Fidget, and he explained how first their client, Ben, had
gone down with the green version, then Emily with the
pink.

'Fortunately,' said Alfred, 'dear Ottoline thought of
everything.'

He opened his safe and took out a small, violent-green
bottle and a small, neon-pink bottle. On both were written:

Two drops to be taken once a lifetime.

'Give the green one to Emily and the pink one to Ben. They should be all right in a matter of moments, though there are side effects.'

'Like what?' said Fidget, carefully putting the two little bottles in his coat pocket.

'Like being able to float in the air. The effect lasts only a matter of days and in anyone other than a human would hardly be noticeable. Anyway, these are the only cures I know of.'

Fidget had put on his hat and scarf when he remembered that they hadn't had a chance to talk about the shop.

Alfred Twizzell took a book from his desk drawer. On the front cover was written:

Wings & Co
Shop Users' Manual

'Well, peel me a prawn,' said Fidget. 'Does it say anything about lockdown?'

'Let me see,' said Alfred, turning the pages. 'Ah. It says you must keep an eye on the shop in case it has anything to tell you.'

'Such as?' asked Fidget.

'It doesn't say,' said Alfred. 'The magician was, as you know, very forgetful.'

It was late afternoon when Fidget arrived back in Podgy Bottom. He thought he should go and see if the shop had anything to tell him. The alleyway where it stood looked, in the gloom, decidedly spooky. The shop was exactly as they'd left it, all boarded up. It seemed to have nothing to say and appeared to be sleeping peacefully.

It's nearly time for ghosties and ghoulies to come out to play, thought Fidget, as he walked along the High Street towards the Red Lion Hotel. He was stopped at the hotel entrance by a group of children dressed as witches and carrying pumpkins.

'Trick or treat?' they cried.

Fidget put on his most frightening expression, the one that made his eyes glow yellow.

'Trick,' he growled.

The children screamed and ran away.

Fidget smiled. This is the one night of the year when I fit in like a mouse in a fur-lined glove, he thought to himself.

It was coming up to six o'clock when Fidget opened the door of the Atlantic Suite to find Emily on the phone.

'Thank you, Alex, that's really helpful. Detective Cardwell should be there any minute. Bye.'

'Where is everyone?' said Fidget. 'What in a frying pan of sprats is going on?'

'It appears that Detective Poppy Perkins and the magic lamp have been captured by the broomstick. James, Buster and Doughnut are on their way to the lock-up garage now. Oh, Fidget, I think this is all my fault. If only I didn't have harpeasles.'

'Hold that haddock, my little ducks,' said Fidget, taking the two bottles out of his pocket. 'Help is at paw.'

Chapter Twenty-Five

In a very long and eventful life, Herbie Snivelle had never for a moment imagined himself holed up in a rabbit hole. Not that this was any old rabbit hole. It had a sitting room, two bedrooms, a hop-in wardrobe, a kitchen and a bathroom. It was, he had to admit, one very comfortable place to stay. And cheap. Herbie liked cheap, unless someone else was paying. Better still, there was no end
of rabbits to help around the hole.

'Carrot juice for two,' bellowed Harpella at the rabbit who was her personal assistant. It hopped away with the order.

'You don't have nothin' stronger, Chicken?' Herbie asked.

'Put ginger in it,' Harpella shouted after the bunny's disappearing tail.

'Chicken,' said Herbie, 'exactly how many rabbits do you have working for you down in this burrow?'

'I don't know. They keep multiplying.'

Harpella was sitting in a comfy armchair in front of the fire while another rabbit massaged her paws.

'There have to be some perks in being a bunny,' she said. 'It wasn't always this easy, but now they think I am their chief.'

The PA rabbit reappeared with two tall glasses of carrot juice.

Herbie regarded them sadly. 'This ain't my scene, Chicken,' he said. 'I need the city streets, the bright lights, the razzamatazz. I'm not cut out for this fresh-air kinda life.'

Harpella's look made his words crumble to dust.

'Let's go through the plans one more time,' said Harpella. 'And don't forget anything.'

'OK,' said Herbie. 'Bout seven, the stretch limo picks us up from Mr Montgomery's farm down the road.'

'Already you have missed the vital bit.'

'I have?'

'Yes, you numbskull. First I get dressed and you make sure I look my very best.'

'Yep, yep, that goes without saying,' said Herbie. He was beginning to feel hot under the collar. 'We're driven to the Red Lion Hotel where . . .' He stopped and smirked. 'Here comes the best bit: I get to shrink the stretch limo.'

'Yes, yes. What do you do in the ballroom?'

'Simple, Chicken. I grab your broomstick, give it to you, you change back into the witch you're meant to be and I skedaddle.'

Harpella kicked the masseuse bunny out of the way, stood up and boxed Herbie round the ears.

'You what?' she said.

'Slip of the tongue, babe. I meant we skedaddle. To our happy-ever-after.'

By seven o'clock that evening, Herbie had come up with a foolproof means of escape. With the matchboxed stretch limo safe in his pocket, he'd slip out of the ballroom while Harpella was busy wrestling with the broomstick. Then it was just a matter of breaking into Wings & Co and smashing up the curious cabinets until he found his wings. Maybe he'd see if he could find his little baby girl's wings too. It would be cute to see what she looked like after all these years. Perhaps she'd missed her daddy.

Harpella stood waiting for Herbie by the entrance to the burrow. All the rabbits had lined up to wave their chief goodbye.

'How do I look?' said Harpella to Herbie. 'I had a few of the rabbits alter the orange cocktail dress to fit a little bit better.'

Herbie thought she looked more frightening than she had before, if that was possible.

'Pretty witchy,' he said.

'Good,' said Harpella.

The walk across the ploughed field was harder for Herbie than for Harpella, who, being a rabbit, had perfect night vision. He could see car headlights in the distance and hear the dogs barking. The stretch limo was waiting in Mr Montgomery's farmyard.

'Put a spurt on, Herbie,' said Harpella, turning up the speed of the Scary Chicken Legs.

Herbie ran after her, cursing.

'My shoes'll be ruined in all this mud,' he said.

'Stop whining,' said Harpella.

By the sound of it, the stretch limo chauffeur was having an argument with the farmer.

'Get out of my yard,' said the farmer. 'I never ordered no fandangling car.'

'Cooee,' called Harpella. Her voice could silence a football stadium. It silenced the dogs, who started to whine at the sight of this extraordinary-looking woman. The electric-orange cocktail dress and purple hair were enough to stop any argument.

'This is our car,' said Harpella. 'Booked in the name of Snivelle.'

'That's right,' said the chauffeur, looking quite scared. 'Don't you live here?'

'No,' said Herbie. 'She has a burrow just across the field.'

'Can't you read?' shouted the farmer. 'The sign says keep out.'

The chauffeur didn't stop to argue. As they drove away, Herbie looked back to see the farmer standing at the gate with his fist raised.

'Next time, I won't just beat him up,' Harpella muttered under her breath.

The sign over the entrance to the Red Lion Hotel read 'A Hallowe'en to Remember'.

'Quite so,' said Harpella.

Mr Flower was standing outside, meeting and greeting his guests. He was dressed as the Demon Rabbit. When he saw the stretch limo pull up, he rushed to open the car door. Herbie had to drag Harpella from the back seat because her chicken legs had seized up.

'Straighten me out,' she hissed.

'That's a winning outfit,' said Mr Flower. 'You looked marvellously scary.'

'You look like a rabbit,' said Harpella.

The hotel manager corrected her. 'A Demon Rabbit.'

'I'll show you demon,' said Harpella. 'Come on, Herbie.'

'Wait,' whispered Herbie. He was still holding onto the limo door.

'Herbie,' she said, 'you can't do anything with the driver still in the car.'

'But, Chicken, you said—'

'Oh, diddums.' Harpella caught his arm in a steel grip. 'Herbie, if you don't stick to the plan you will be VERY SORRY.'

Herbie followed her into the ballroom. The lights were so low that it was impossible to see anyone, let alone a broomstick. Monster music pounded out.

'I hate Hallowe'en,' said Herbie.

Chapter Twenty-Six

Alex had confirmed Buster and James's worst fears: Poppy and the magic lamp had been kidnapped. Alex had taken some photos with his Polaroid camera. They mostly showed little except masses of pink smoke, but in one, Detective Cardwell could make out the ghostly shapes of Poppy and the magic lamp being thrown in the back of a white van.

Buster had tried the door to the lock-up garage. It was unlocked and inside there was nothing to be seen except a mobile phone lying on the floor. James picked it up.

'It's Poppy's,' he said.

He found his Austin Healey parked round the corner from Alex's house. A pencil-written note stuck to the windscreen was addressed to Wings & Co. It read:

If you want to see Poppy Perkins and the magic lamp again, stay away from the Hallowe'en Ball. DD

James showed the note to Buster.

'We can't not go to the ball,' said Buster. 'It's our duty to be there. We have to stop Harpella from getting her broomstick back, especially now she's reunited with Herbie Snivelle. The fairy world is in grave danger. And humans could well get hurt.'

'Yes, yes, I know. Buddleia,' said James. 'Buddleia and bindweed. Now I can't remember where Poppy said she'd leave the car keys. I'm losing the plot.'

'You don't see that little detective on TV – the one with a moustache – lose the plot,' said Buster. 'Do you know why that is?'

'I have a nasty feeling you are going to tell me.'

'Yes, I am,' said Buster. 'It's because he's never in loooooove. Being in love and being a detective don't go together.'

'You're eleven; how could you understand?'

There was an awkward silence between them. Once James had only been a year older than Buster, but he'd grown up while Buster had stayed eleven.

Doughnut sniffed out the keys. Poppy had left them hidden on the front wheel.

'I have an idea,' said Buster. 'It's a Hallowe'en Ball and everyone will be in fancy dress. If we dress up too, how will Doctor Dreadalpan know it's us?'

'Where are we going to get costumes this late in the

day?' said James.

The detectives thought hard then both said together, 'Mr Rollo the tailor.'

'He has connections with the theatre,' said Buster. 'He's bound to be able to lay his hands on something.'

'You know, this is mighty dangerous,' said James, as they drove back to Podgy Bottom. 'Doctor Dreadalpan is out to catch Harpella, and Harpella is out to catch her broomstick. Whoever bumps into the other first, it's not going to be pretty.'

It was dark when they drew up outside the Red Lion Hotel. Mr Rollo had been more than helpful and the car was stuffed with bags.

'"A Hallowe'en to Remember,"' said James, reading the sign over the entrance. 'Why does that instil fear in my heart?'

Buster and Doughnut climbed out of the car.

'I'll go and park,' called James. 'Be with you shortly.'

The first guests were beginning to arrive as Buster, weighed down by the bags, walked into the cobweb-covered foyer. Joan rushed up to him.

'What do you think of my costume?' she asked.

She was dressed in an orange dress with huge wedge shoes that made her look very tall. In addition, she was wearing a purple wig and a witch's nose.

Buster thought that she bore more than a passing resemblance to a certain witch he would rather not ever see again.

'I went into Karen Pin's shop the other day,' explained Joan. 'I had no idea what I was going to wear for the ball, until Karen's mum, Maureen – you know, the one with the yappy dog – said she had seen the best witch ever and gave me the idea.'

'Great,' said Buster.

A rather portly ghost arrived, accompanied by a terrifying witch with wings.

'Sergeant Litton,' said Joan, 'and Mrs Litton . . . welcome!'

Buster made his escape. In the Atlantic Suite, he and Doughnut found Emily completely cured of harpeasles, but unable to keep her feet on the ground. Every time she took a breath she floated towards the ceiling.

'What have you there, young sprat?' said Fidget. Buster was almost hidden among all the bags.

'Hallowe'en costumes. Come on, we need to change, there's not a moment to—' Buster stopped. 'What is Emily doing up there?'

'She's floating. It's a side effect of the cure for harpeasles. The spots have gone.'

'Great. How does she intend to get down?'

'I can hear you,' said Emily.

'Then you might like to know that your friend Alex is covered in green spots. Another human who thinks he can be a detective.'

Emily was suddenly so filled with rage that she came down to the floor with a bump.

'You are horrid,' she said. 'If it wasn't for Alex—'

Buster laughed. 'Works every time. Rage is so heavy, you see, it stops you floating.'

Fidget had pulled some costumes out of the bags. He held up a pumpkin.

'What's this for?' he asked.

Emily rose from the floor again and banged her head on the chandelier.

'Oh dear,' she said. 'It's a bit like having hiccups.'

'It's for Emily to wear at the Hallowe'en Ball,' said Buster.

'But I'll just float away in that,' said Emily. 'Like a helium balloon.'

'No great loss,' said Buster.

'You are so rude,' said Emily crossly, and returned to the floor again.

Buster chuckled.

'Wait a minnow,' said Fidget. 'Since when have we been going to the Hallowe'en Ball?'

'Since we found this,' said Buster, and showed Fidget the note that had been left on James's car. 'Where's Ben?'

'On top of the wardrobe in his bedroom,' said Fidget.

'How long does this side effect last?'

'Only a matter of days, Alfred Twizzell thought,' said Fidget.

Buster pulled out the other costumes and gave one to Fidget. It was furry with a snout and bloody fangs.

'This should fit you,' he said.

'What is it?' asked Fidget.

'A werewolf, of course,' said Buster. 'No time for complaints. A floating pumpkin and a werewolf will fit in fine. After all, the unofficial guest list for the Hallowe'en Ball includes one broomstick, previously an alchemist–'

'Alchemist-stroke-wizard,' interrupted Fidget.

'One broomstick, previously an alchemist-stroke-wizard,' continued Buster, 'out for revenge; a bunny, previously a witch, who wants her broomstick back; a thug with a nasty little habit of shrinking cars, previously the witch's husband, and I suspect they are all about to turn up downstairs.'

'Well, slap me with a kipper,' said Fidget, and zipped up his werewolf suit.

Emily had just put on her pumpkin costume when her mobile rang. She managed to grab it before she floated away.

'Hello,' she said. 'It's Mr Gravel,' she whispered to Fidget and Buster. Fidget pulled Emily down to the sofa with his paw and held her there.

'You mean Gravel as in Grim and Gravel?' said Buster. 'Ask him what they've done with Poppy and the magic lamp. And put him on speaker phone.'

Emily nodded. 'How are you, Mr Gravel?' she said.

'That's the thing,' said Gravel. 'I'm not well. I've come out in pink spots.'

'I'm so sorry. It's harpeasles. You must have caught it from me,' said Emily.

'Oh – thanks a bunch. But, listen, you said you worked for a fairy detective agency – is that right?'

'Yes,' said Emily.

There was silence on the line and just when she thought Gravel might have hung up, he said, 'It's not some kids' game?'

'No, not at all,' said Emily. 'We investigate fairy meddling.'

'Like?'

'Like the broomstick who goes by the name of Doctor Dreadalpan.'

'Look, you're a bright girl, but is there a grown-up at your detective agency who I could talk to?'

'Yes,' said Emily.

'Not the coppers, right?'

'Don't worry. Fidget is a cat.'

'A . . . cat . . .' said Gravel.

He definitely didn't sound very well. Fidget took the phone.

'Hello, Mr Gravel. Can I help?'

'You see,' Fidget heard Gravel take a deep breath. 'You see, there was this detective lady and the boss, that is, Doctor Dreadalpan . . . er . . . caught her snooping about. He told us to put her in the van. She had a lamp with her – I think it was an electronic toy of some sort, like they make at the Scarycrow factory. But we couldn't find the Off button.'

'It doesn't have one, unfortunately,' said Fidget.

'I had to stuff its spout with paper to stop it from babbling on and on.'

'We all feel like doing that from time to time.'

'But the thing is, mate, the detective lady, she was tied up tighter than a Christmas present. I mean, she wasn't going anywhere and then there was all this blue smoke and she was gone, just gone.'

'Batter me a haddock,' said Fidget, sitting up. 'That's very interesting.'

'And there's something else,' said Gravel. 'It wasn't me who done the bank. It was the boss. I just drove the van.'

'Done what bank?' said Fidget. He looked at Buster, who was making frantic gestures with his arms. 'Tell me more about the bank, Mr Gravel.'

'Look, I've got to go, I'm not feeling well,' said Gravel. 'But Doctor Dreadalpan is on his way to the Red Lion Hotel. And it won't be just the one broomstick at the ball.'

'Mr Gravel,' said Fidget, as solemn as a salmon. 'Just a moment . . .'

But he'd hung up.

Emily floated over to the Think Board and moved the strings about.

Nearly everyone on the board seemed to be heading in one direction – to the Red Lion Hotel.

Ben wafted into the sitting room dressed as a ghost. 'I should really be downstairs at the ball promoting Scarycrow,' he said.

'Great outfit, Ben. It really works with that floating thing you've got going,' said Buster. He guided Ben back to his bedroom. 'We'll be going down any minute. Here's James now.'

'Buster, is that you in there?' said James.

Buster was dressed as a bumblebee with a large, round tummy and false wings.

'Yes, it's me,' said Buster, taking off his mask.

'What am I going to wear?' asked James.

'This is the only costume that'll fit you,' said Buster. 'You're going as Count Dracula.'

Chapter Twenty-Seven

Grim was wearing his skeleton outfit and his bones were aching. He drove up to the side entrance of the Red Lion Hotel, where he parked the van just across from the car park.

'I'm not feeling very well, Boss,' he said to the broomstick.

The broomstick studied Grim. Like Gravel earlier, Grim had come out in spots. His spots were green. The broomstick jumped out of the van and took in its surroundings. Above it was the hotel's wrought-iron fire escape. Next to where the van was parked were two large rubbish bins, and next to them was the ballroom's fire exit.

Grim opened the back of the van. Inside was all the money from the bank robbery, thirty broomsticks and a couple of electronic toys. Grim unloaded the broomsticks and they stood in a row awaiting orders. They gave Grim the creeps. The boss silently forced open the fire exit door and waved them into the ballroom.

Grim was about to follow when the boss stopped him. It took out a 2B pencil and wrote the word SCARPER on the side of the van.

Grim couldn't believe his luck.

'You mean go home?'

The broomstick nodded.

Grim was about to ask about the money and then thought better of it. He realised he had never in his whole life been so happy to leave anything as he was to leave the boss and the money behind. He would forget the whole sorry business and go to bed with a hot water bottle and a glass of milk. But first, he thought, he would make an anonymous call to the police and tell them what was going on. Someone needed to find out what had happened to that lady detective. As he reached the main road, he looked back and saw the boss throw something shiny high into the air. It landed with a thump in the rubbish bin.

'This ball will put the Red Lion Hotel back on the map,' said Mr Flower to Joan.

'It's completely sold out,' said Joan, adjusting her purple wig. 'I do think it was a stomping idea to hire

Shivers & Slithers.' The band had just started playing. Shivers & Slithers' hip-hop horror hullabaloo was already shaking the building. 'And the other acts promise to be just as good.'

There was to be a fire-eater, a spooky magician, and Siouxsie Swift, the runner-up in The Me Moment TV show, was going to hand out a prize for the best Hallowe'en costume of the night. So far, thought Mr Flower, the lady with the chicken legs looked as if she'd win by a mile.

'This,' he said, rubbing his hands together with glee, 'is definitely going to be a night to remember.'

Herbie Snivelle was in a sulk, mainly because Harpella hadn't let him shrink the stretch limo, but also because she had his hand in a steel-like grip so he couldn't escape.

Shivers & Slithers had just launched into their 1970s smash hit 'Monster Murder' when the fairy detectives and Ben arrived in the ballroom. Poor Doughnut had bravely stayed behind in the Atlantic Suite to protect the keys. He wasn't too keen on being alone. Dachshunds like company but, quite frankly, seventeen keys were not the kind of company Doughnut had in mind. Doughnut wasn't very good at counting but shortly after the others left, it seemed to him that one of the keys was missing. Doughnut hadn't a dog's dinner of an idea what he was supposed to do. In desperation he did the only thing he could do – he started barking.

Several people were now on the dance floor, much to Harpella's annoyance, for they kept bumping into her. She hated people touching her. Herbie was relieved when he finally spied the broomstick.

'Over there, Chicken,' he said.

'Where?' hissed Harpella.

'There,' said Herbie. 'No, there . . . and there . . . and there . . .' There were broomsticks everywhere. He had never seen so many broomsticks in one ballroom. 'Which is yours, Chicken?'

'I don't know,' said Harpella. 'But I will find it if it is the last thing I do.'

Ben saw his Scary Chicken Legs striding about the dance floor and, having very little memory of the truly terrifying rabbit operating them, floated up to Harpella.

'Those are my Scary Chicken Legs,' he said, and found himself on the ceiling.

'You'll stay up there,' shouted Harpella, 'if you know what's good for you.'

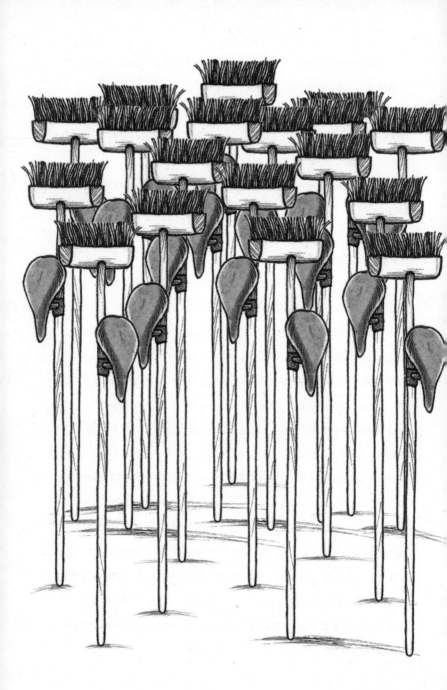

Sergeant Litton had just received a call from the police station. Unfortunately, he could hardly hear a word.

'Dumpty, put the phone away,' said his mother. 'How many times do I have to tell you? It's rude to speak on the phone when you're out with Mumsie.'

'But, Mumsie, it could be important,' said Sergeant Litton.

His mother was having none of it. She grabbed the phone and put it in her evening bag, closing it with a menacing snap. So Sergeant Litton never heard what it was that Grim had called the station to say.

The arrival of the broomsticks sent Harpella into a frenzy. Inside the robot costume she couldn't see at all well. Herbie was trying to collect as many of them as he could, which was proving darn difficult, for each broomstick put up a terrible fight. And then, to add to Harpella's fury, she caught sight of a suspicious-looking pumpkin. That, she thought, is Emily Vole. Pumpkin or no pumpkin, she can't fool me. Where, Harpella wondered, as she tried to look around, were the rest of the loathsome fairy detectives? She'd had enough of the robot head. She ripped it off and sent it flying across the ballroom where it landed in front of Joan. Joan screamed, as did many who saw the purple rabbit head sticking out of an orange cocktail dress.

Emily, seeing Harpella rushing towards her with her robot arms outstretched, thought of the happiest thing she could and floated out of her grasp. A second later Emily had joined Ben and had a perfect view of the ballroom. The guests applauded, thinking it was all a part of the show and Mrs Litton congratulated Mr Flower on the high standard of the hotel's Hallowe'en performers.

Fidget knew that somehow he had to get Harpella out of there. Fairy meddling and humans very rarely mixed. He was working his way across the dance floor when he felt a tap on his shoulder.

'Mr Fidget? Or should I say Mr Werewolf?' said Joan, towering over him. 'I'm sorry, but your piranha is barking.'

'Buddleia,' said Fidget. 'What's happened now?'

As he left the ballroom, he saw Count Dracula.

'Is everything all right?' the count whispered to the werewolf.

'It's Doughnut. I'll be back in a mo. Buddleia, look at all those broomsticks.'

'I'm on it,' said Dracula.

Fidget could hear Doughnut before the lift doors opened. He spoke only basic Dog but you didn't need to understand much to know what Doughnut was saying.

'Help, help. I need help.'

Cautiously, Fidget opened the door to the suite. To his surprise he saw the keys were all sitting quietly on the sofa. All . . . sixteen of them . . .

'Buddleia and bindweed,' said Fidget. 'This is no time to be bringing fairies back to collect their wings.'

It was then that the fire alarm went off. There was nothing else to do except put the sixteen keys in Emily's satchel and, carrying Doughnut, run down the wrought-iron fire escape.

The guests were streaming out into the car park. Most of them had thought it was part of the act when a shower of sparks had shot out of a broomstick's bristles, followed by clouds of pink smoke. In the distance, the sound of fire engines' sirens could be heard. That was when things took a turn for the worse.

Chapter Twenty-Eight

Two fire engines arrived outside the Red Lion Hotel, their blue lights flashing. Herbie didn't waste a moment. Here was the chance he'd been longing for. Harpella, the broomsticks and all the other guests flooded out into the car park. Even though she towered over everyone in her Scary Chicken Legs, Harpella didn't notice him sneaking off. She had her mind set on one thing and one thing only: getting her broomstick back.

'Doctor Dreadalpan, show yourself, you coward,' she shouted.

It is a strange thing, but if someone has bullied you, no matter how long ago, you still have that little tinge of fear that makes you do what they say. One of the broomsticks glided slightly towards her.

'How could I not have recognised you?' she said. Harpella kicked off the Scary Chicken Legs and jumped out of the robot. She sank her rabbit teeth into the wood of the broomstick's handle.

The werewolf was with the bumblebee at the foot of the fire escape, Doughnut at his heels and the sixteen keys safe in Emily's satchel. Emily and Ben floated out of the ballroom window and on to the fire escape. As they clung there, Emily saw Herbie running towards the fire engines, his water pistol in his hand.

She shouted to Fidget and Buster. 'Look, Herbie's going for the fire engines. Quick, do something before he shrinks them.'

'I see him, my little ducks,' said Fidget, handing the satchel to Buster. 'I'll show that barnacled bottom-feeder who's past it.'

He threw back the werewolf head and pushed through the crowd to where the Scary Chicken Legs lay abandoned on the ground. He climbed into them and after a few false starts set off after Herbie at an alarming speed.

The guests weren't sure which way to turn. Should they follow the werewolf with the cat's head and the Scary Chicken Legs? Or continue to watch the wrestling match between the purple rabbit and the broomstick?

Mr Flower felt it his duty to make an announcement.

In a shaky voice, he said, 'It was a false alarm, ladies and gentlemen. Will everyone please go back into the ballroom?'

No one moved, not until the broomstick swept several of the guests aside and, nearly knocking over Mr Flower, flew past him dragging the purple rabbit in his wake, Count Dracula and the bumblebee in hot pursuit.

The guests cheered and followed. They didn't want to miss the show, it was so much fun.

'A brilliant idea,' said the Mr Phipps to Mr Flower. 'Promenade theatre – very modern. I'd put money on the broomstick.'

Emily, holding tight to the rail, made her way down the fire escape.

'Best you float back in through the window,' she called to Ben. 'I'll see if I can get to Fidget.'

It was just as she reached the bottom that she heard a mournful cry coming from one of the big rubbish bins.

'Help, oh, help. Someone help me, pleeeease.'

'Oh dear,' said Emily.

'What are you doing floating about out here?' said the bumblebee from the fire exit door. 'Trying to learn to fly?'

'Oh, put a sock in it,' said Emily, and was perfectly grounded again. 'The magic lamp is in the rubbish bin.'

'It can stay there,' said Buster. 'I'm not going to climb up and pull it out.'

'You could fly,' said Emily.

'I can't, actually,' said Buster. 'If you haven't noticed, I am dressed as a bumblebee and my wings are pinned down.'

Emily sighed, took a deep breath and tried to stop being cross with Buster. Holding her nose, she floated up just high enough to peer over the top of the bin. With her other hand she pulled out the lamp. It was covered in pumpkin seeds and potato peelings. With some difficulty she floated down to where Buster was waiting and held on to his arm.

'Oh, sweet mistress, I have been abused,' said the lamp. 'Abused, I tell you.'

'What happened to Poppy?' asked Buster.

'Have you a hanky?' said the magic lamp.

'No,' said Buster. 'I'm eleven and no eleven-year-old has a hanky.'

He was desperate to go back into the ballroom.

'I need to go to our suite and have a proper bath in Brasso,' said the lamp. 'And forgive me, sweet mistress, but pumpkin is not your colour.'

'Where's Poppy?' said Emily.

'How should I know? I've been in a rubbish bin. I'll tell you everything when I'm clean.'

'All you ever think about is yourself,' said Emily. 'There are more important things than you being a bit smelly.'

'Sweet mistress, don't be like that! You don't understand . . .'

'And you don't understand that we have to stop Harpella getting her broomstick back.'

'That broomstick was the source of all my woes. It was the broomstick who . . .'

'Oh, forget it,' said Emily. 'What are we waiting for, Buster? We have work to do.'

Leaving the lamp by the rubbish bins, the very cross pumpkin and the bumblebee went back into the ballroom.

'What about me?' wailed the magic lamp.

No one understood. It'd had to put up with so much; first the humiliation at the theatre, now this abuse at the hands of the broomstick. Perhaps it was all over for the magic lamp. Perhaps it was just a useless piece of junk. But perhaps . . .

The magic lamp pushed open the fire exit door and trotted purposefully through the legs of the guests into the ballroom.

The pumpkin and the bumblebee found Count Dracula in the crowd round the broomstick and the bunny. The broomstick had Harpella in a bunny headlock. She was thumping her hind legs on the ballroom floor. Half the broomstick's bristles were missing. As the guests stamped and cheered, the magic lamp tapped the broomstick on the saddle.

The fight stopped and the room went quiet.

'You?' said Harpella. She jumped up and grabbed the magic lamp between her paws. 'You, you cheating piece of cheap ironmongery.'

'Oh, buddleia,' said James. 'What is the magic lamp thinking?'

The other thirty broomsticks lined up behind their boss.

'Change me back,' said Harpella to the broomstick.

It waved its arms and sparks flew across the dance floor.

'Change me back into the witch I always was and I will remove the curse I put on you.' Her soft bunny eyes became whirlpools. 'Promise, pretty promise.'

It seemed that the broomstick was about to obey when Fidget, half-cat, half-werewolf, crashed through the ballroom doors, wobbling on the Scary Chicken Legs. He had hold of Herbie Snivelle, who was clutching a matchbox.

'Lemme,' he whined. 'Lemme shrink the fire engine.'

Too late, Fidget realised that the Scary Chicken Legs were out of control and they were heading at full speed towards Harpella and the broomsticks. He let go of Herbie and leapt as only a cat can, landing well away from the oncoming collision. Herbie, Harpella, thirty-one broomsticks and the magic lamp exploded in an eruption of multi-coloured sparks and purple smoke.

There was a moment of stunned silence. The guests watched as the huge, purple rabbit with pink ears emerged bewildered from the clouds of smoke. She hopped from the ballroom, through the foyer and out of the hotel into the night, followed by an equally big blue rabbit, a fedora hat perched between his purple ears, a matchbox held between his rabbit teeth.

When the smoke finally cleared, there, amid thirty lifeless broomsticks, stood a man dressed in Elizabethan costume. His long face was not unlike a bicycle saddle. He was tall and his bristly white hair stuck up on his head like a brush. He wore a flowing gown of midnight blue and in his gloved hands he held the magic lamp.

The audience went wild. What a show! Doctor Dreadalpan took a bow and put the magic lamp on the floor.

'More!' shouted the guests.

Doctor Dreadalpan and the magic lamp took another bow. Just for a second the magic lamp forgot its woes, the applause taking it back to its winning performance on The Me Moment TV show when its future had looked bright.

'Show's over,' said a stunned Mr Flower, not quite sure what had just happened.

'Hold on a mo,' said Fidget to Doctor Dreadalpan, who was gliding towards the exit.

'Where do you think you're going?' said James.

'Away. And if you or anyone else tries to stop me, I'll broomstick the lot of you.'

'Tell me where Poppy Perkins is,' said James.

Doctor Dreadalpan looked at James Cardwell and laughed a nasty laugh.

'You are a detective, are you not?' he said. 'Then find her.' And with that and a whoosh, he was gone.

Chapter Twenty-Nine

The magic lamp wandered off into the night, forgotten.

'Forgotten!' it said to itself. 'After I risked everything to prevent the worst from happening, after I prevented Harpella from becoming a witch again, my sweet mistress has forgotten me.'

The lamp had to admit it was slightly unfortunate about Doctor Dreadalpan. But close-up magic is pretty tricky at the best of times, and when you're feeling smelly and unloved it's very hard indeed.

It was well past the witching hour. The magic lamp stood on the High Street, watching the guests spill out of the Red Lion Hotel, and sighed. They would never know, the lamp thought, what fairy mischief might have been unleashed on them if it hadn't been for me.

It turned its handle towards the hotel and walked off into the dark night of the crumpled teacake. The magic lamp had to face the bare, un-Brassoed truth: the stage had sent it packing, the broomstick had abused it and Emily was fed up with it. The magic lamp was never recognised for the noble ironmongery it was. Ignored, pushed aside, left on props tables, thrown in rubbish bins . . . FORGOTTEN. A tear rolled down its round belly. So lost was it in the woe of its days that at first it didn't hear someone calling.

'Wait, magic lamp, wait!'

It was a voice it knew. The lamp turned round to see Poppy running down the street after it.

'You're all covered in pumpkin seeds,' said Poppy. 'What happened?'

'Oh, nothing to make a fuss about. Just thrown into a rubbish bin.'

'Come along,' said Poppy. 'James and the others are in terrible danger.'

'No, they're not,' said the magic lamp.

'Come on,' said Poppy, trying to take the magic lamp's hand. 'We must go to the Red Lion, quickly.'

The magic lamp held tightly to a street lamp and refused to move. 'I'm not going back,' wailed the woebegone lamp.

'Why not?' said Poppy.

'I . . . I . . . I feel faint,' said the magic lamp, and so saying, flopped spout-down in a puddle.

When it came to, the magic lamp found itself in a small brightly lit cafe at the all-night petrol station. On a plate before it were a toasted teacake and a mug of hot chocolate with whipped cream on top.

'Try and eat a little,' said Poppy.

'I can't,' said the magic lamp, pushing the plate away. 'I'm off my food.'

Poppy pushed the plate back again.

'For me – please,' she said. The magic lamp took a small bite of the teacake, then another and another. 'Now tell me,' said Poppy, 'is James . . . are the others all right?'

'Oh, they're fine,' said the lamp, suddenly feeling much better.

'What about Doctor Dreadalpan? Do you know where he is?'

'Let's just say he is no longer a broomstick. More a stick-thin wizard. I did that.'

'You did?' said Poppy. 'That was brave of you. How did you do it?'

The magic lamp ate a little bit more and drank a little bit more and began to feel its spirit lighten.

'Well, it was like this . . .' And the magic lamp told Poppy all that had happened.

'Do you really think I'm brave?' said the magic lamp, when it had finished.

'Yes,' said Poppy.

'Good. Now, what happened to you?' said the magic lamp.

'I was in the van with you, trussed up as tight as a turkey, when it filled with blue smoke. I couldn't see anything. I called out to you but then the smoke cleared and I found I was no longer in the van but in a very old shop. I felt all tingly and I knew that I had my wings back.'

Poppy stood up and gave her wings a twirl.

'They're baby wings,' said the magic lamp.

'Yes, my dad handed them in when I was tiny,' said Poppy. 'You know, I think we should tell the others we're OK.'

'Wait a mo,' said the magic lamp. 'If you had your wings back, why didn't you fly to the hotel?'

'I couldn't,' said Poppy. 'I was still trussed up. But the key showed me the way to the kitchen. I rolled and bumped down the stairs and there I managed to cut the rope on an ancient tin opener on the wall.'

'You have a key with you?' said the magic lamp. 'Which one?' Poppy took a key out of her pocket and set it down on the table. 'Cyril!' cried the lamp. 'Cyril, my dear friend!' Cyril fluttered onto the lamp's outstretched arm.

'I couldn't find my mobile,' continued Poppy. 'The shop

phone wasn't working and neither were the lights. The front door refused to open, and the windows and the back door wouldn't budge. I was stuck. Fortunately I found a candle and some matches and there were lots of tins of sardines in the larder so I didn't go hungry. Then suddenly, all the lights came on and the front door swung open.'

'The shop has unlocked itself?' said the magic lamp. 'Yippee!' It jumped up and clicked its Moroccan-slippered heels together. 'Then that's where we should go, not back to the hotel.'

'But I should call James from the payphone here.'

'No need,' said the magic lamp. 'They'll all be at the shop faster than you can say, "Genie, grant me a wish."'

Poppy and the magic lamp walked together through

the deserted town, occasionally passing a weary ghost or ghoulie on his way home from a party. Finally, they came to the alleyway where Wings & Co's shop stood. Both were thrilled to see a light on in every window and the door open, waiting for them.

'Yoo hoo,' called the magic lamp, running into the shop. 'I'm ba-ack.'

'They're not here,' said Poppy sadly.

'Don't worry, they will be,' said the magic lamp. 'I'm going upstairs to have a wash and a shine.'

Poppy was trying to call James on the shop phone when she looked up to see him walking briskly down the alleyway. Without a second thought, she ran to him.

'Poppy! Thank the old Faerie Queene you're safe,' said James. 'I have been so worried about you . . .' He stopped, all red and embarrassed. 'I . . . I know you're a fairy,' said James.

Poppy put her arms round him and kissed him.

'I've always known you were a fairy,' said Poppy. 'But I have baby wings, look, not proper ones like yours.'

'They're beautiful,' said James, kissing her. 'Just like you, quite beautiful.'

'Oh no,' said Buster, appearing behind James with Fidget, Emily and Doughnut. 'That's really gross. It's what they do in movies, just at the end when it's been quite good up to that point and it always spoils everything.'

Chapter Thirty

Buster was of the opinion that this grown-up love
business was very overrated.

'This is not the time to be all soppy,' he said. 'There are
a lot of loose ends to be tied up.'

Everyone was sitting round the kitchen table while
Fidget made them a very late supper. Or possibly a very
early breakfast. Emily had discovered that she only needed
to look at Buster to feel quite cross so she was having no
trouble at all staying in her seat.

'Like what?' said James, staring dreamily at Poppy.

'Like de-pumpkinating Miss Pin's mother and her dog.
Like finding out what happened to the stolen money from
the bank robbery. Like de-harpeasling Grim and Gravel
before everyone in Podgy Bottom comes out in spots.'

'Spot on the fishcake,' said Fidget, putting a huge
platter of them in the middle of the table.

'And,' added Buster, 'like telling Poppy that her dad,
Herbie Snivelle, is the only big blue rabbit in the fairy world

with a fine collection of matchbox-sized cars.'

'What?' said Poppy.

'Buster!' shouted Emily and James together.

'What's the problem?' said Buster. 'Someone had to tell her.'

'Yes,' said Emily, 'but there was no need to be so tactless.'

'Hold that halibut,' said Fidget. 'I knew Pete Perkins; he was a fisherman. Poppy's mother is a postmistress in Porlock and makes the best pollock pie I've ever tasted. Isn't that right, Poppy?'

'Yes,' said Poppy. 'And it's lovely to meet you at last. Mum often talks about you. She'll be thrilled to hear I've got my wings back.'

'You're the spitting image of her, if I may say so. Pretty as pilchards, both of you. Honestly, Buster, what made you think Poppy was the only baby whose wings were left here?'

'Don't look at me like that,' said Buster. 'James thought she was Herbie's daughter, and Emily did too, didn't you?'

'Yes, but unlike you I didn't go blurting it out,' said Emily. 'We hadn't any proof, remember?'

'OK, sorry,' said Buster. 'Enough with the kissing and canoodling please,' he added as James kissed Poppy again. 'Remember I'm only eleven and Emily is nine. Show some respect for our tender years.'

Fidget clapped his paws together. 'Eat up, then everyone needs to be fish-shaped and orderly. We have magic to work.'

'Magic? Did I hear someone call my name?' Shining like new, the magic lamp, with an escort of keys, came down the stairs to a round of applause.

'Yes, there are still some fish to fry,' said Fidget. 'But we should be able to finish the job before it gets light. After all, we are Wings & Co. Magic lamp, perhaps you would start by making this safe.'

Fidget laid Herbie's big, plastic water pistol on the table.

Karen Pin never found out what had happened to her mum and Hellman, or where they'd been. They both turned up in the early hours of the morning after Hallowe'en. Her mother looked as if she'd spent too long on a sun-bed but she seemed a much happier person after her experience, whatever it was, and Hellman was much calmer. Maureen Pin went back to live in her own flat and decided to go travelling with her dog and see the world.

The white van was on Mr Phibbs' forecourt when he arrived to open up his car showroom that morning. The van was quite empty but tucked under a windscreen wiper was a pencil-written note. It was addressed to Sergeant Litton and read:

Thank the bank for the unsecured loan.
DD

Emily phoned Alex and told him she'd pop over to see him that afternoon and return his Polaroid photos. She had just the thing to cure his spots – and loads to tell him.

Grim and Gravel too found themselves completely cured of their spots, though they'd both had strange dreams of being given medicine by a man-sized cat. They felt much better than they had done in ages, and the petty crooks decided to hand themselves in to the police. After what they'd been through, a spell in prison would seem like a holiday. It was only when they got to the bus stop that they realised something wasn't right. The wind blew and the next thing they knew they were carried away, floating high over the rooftops and fields. Try as they might they couldn't make themselves go down to earth and they were never seen in Podgy Bottom again. In case you are wondering, Grim and Gravel landed safely in a field in foreign parts. A clean start beckoned; no more crooked stuff for them. They became as good as gold.

That afternoon Detectives Cardwell and Perkins drove back to Scotland Yard to report on the outcome of their investigation of the Matchbox Mysteries.

'Unfortunately, sir,' said James to the Detective Chief Inspector, 'we were unable to apprehend the villain. He has . . . er . . . gone to ground. But believe me, no one would want the life he has now.'

'And it's not possible to restore the vehicles to their owners?' asked the DCI.

'No,' said Poppy. 'Once a car has been shrunk to matchbox size there is very little one can do to resize it.'

The DCI looked long and hard at the two detectives standing in front of his desk.

'A pity,' he said at last and closed the file. 'You are quite certain that this car-shrinking won't happen again?'

James placed Herbie's water pistol on the DCI's desk. 'Be assured, sir, the villain is now non-operational.'

That evening James and Poppy stood on a high window ledge at Scotland Yard, looking out over London as the sun set on the river and autumn leaves fluttered to the pavement below.

'Beautiful,' said James. He took Poppy's hand and they flew off to supper together.

It turned out to be the best Hallowe'en ever for Ben's company. After seeing the Scary Chicken Legs' performance at the ball, the head buyer at Martin's department store ordered as many pairs as Scarycrow could make by Christmas.

And that was that. Until one day Fidget received a postcard. On the front was a very good drawing of a broomstick. On the back, written in pencil, were the words:

I will see you again.
DD

FIN

Spot on the fishcake.

Welcome to the famous fairy detective agency,
Wings & Co. There's talking cat Fidget, grumpy
fairy detective Buster Ignatius Spicer, who's been
eleven for a hundred years, a bossy magic lamp,
and orphan Emily Vole, who was discovered in
a hatbox at Stansted Airport.

Together they solve the crimes no other detectives can
tackle – a plague of bunnies, some mysteriously missing
luck and one very large, very lost giant.

Squat on a squid, you won't want to skip a single
Wings & Co adventure.

www.orionbooks.co.uk

the
orion star

CALLING ALL GROWN-UPS!
Sign up for **the orion star** newsletter to
hear about your favourite authors and exclusive
competitions, plus details of how children
can join our 'Story Stars' review panel.

Sign up at:

www.orionbooks.co.uk/orionstar

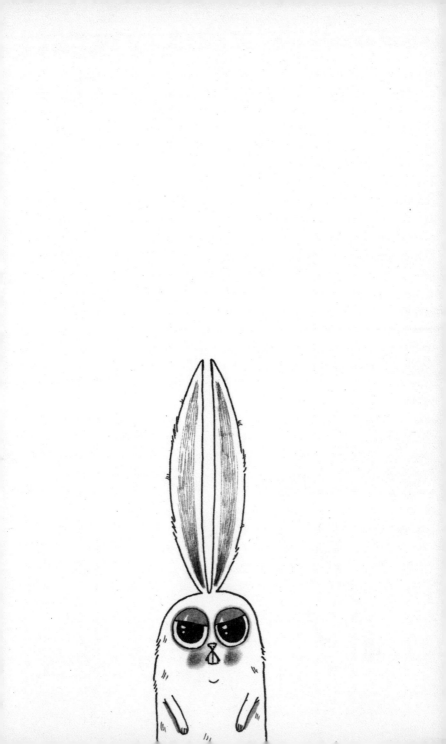